Charis was drenched by the rainstorm

Rafe drew her under a tree. "You're shivering," he said with concern. "Have you anything else to wear in here?" he demanded, drawing the rucksack off his shoulder.

"There's a sweater. I could put that on."

"Not over that wet sun top," he told her tersely. "Take it off."

"Oh, but I ca—" She broke off, embarrassed that she wasn't wearing a bra.

"If you're trying to tell me you haven't got anything on underneath, I can see that for myself," he told her dryly.

Charis blushed, and instinctively her hands went up to cover herself. But Rafe said, "Don't be silly," and reached over and pulled the top slowly over her head. Charis couldn't speak, couldn't move. His eyes met hers. Then, very deliberately, he kissed her on the mouth, then bent his head and kissed each breast.

SALLY WENTWORTH

man for hire

Harlequin Books

TORONTO • NEW YORK • LOS ANGELES • LONDON
AMSTERDAM • PARIS • SYDNEY • HAMBURG
STOCKHOLM • ATHENS • TOKYO • MILAN

Harlequin Presents first edition December 1982
ISBN 0-373-10557-6

Original hardcover edition published in 1982
by Mills & Boon Limited

CHAPTER ONE

CHARIS RADCLIFFE picked up the newspaper and read the item in the personal column yet again. There were only a few lines and she had already read them so often that she could probably have quoted them off by heart, but she went over each word again carefully, as if they could tell her something new, then she sat back and pensively drew a ring round the item. It read: 'Ex-Army officer (Major), presentable, articulate. Para. 8 years. OP. Mngt. Exp. Europe and mid-East. Exemp. record. Prepared to travel. Requires honest, short term employment. Write Box No. BB.106.'

She could only guess that OP. Mngt. meant that the advertiser had experience of operations management, whatever that might signify in the modern-day Army, but the rest was clear enough, or at least as clear as one could be in a six-line advert. Even so, Charis still bit the end of her pen for several minutes before at last putting a sheet of blank paper in the typewriter and decisively beginning to write. 'Dear Sir, I have read your advert in today's *Daily Messenger*, and may be able to offer you some employment which might be of interest to you. If your services are still available will you please reply to J. Smith, c/o Carter, Davis (Solicitors), 21 Grey's Terrace, S.W.1., giving a place and time for a meeting, in London, as soon as possible.'

Short and businesslike, just like the advert. Quickly

Charis scrawled a signature on the bottom which might just possibly have been deciphered as J. Smith and hastily sealed and addressed the envelope before she could change her mind.

'Working in your lunch hour?'

Charis jumped guiltily as one of the partners breezed into the office, pushing the door with 'Carter, Davis, Solicitors' painted on it in gold letters shut behind him. Before she had time to deny it, he went on, 'Any messages?'

'No, it's been very quiet.'

He walked through to his own office and Charis slipped the letter among others waiting to be put through the franking machine and taken to be posted. The letter should arrive at its destination early tomorrow morning and, with any luck, the ex-army officer would collect it the same day. Then would come the trying wait to see if he would send a reply to J. Smith; a letter Charis would quietly extract from the pile of other correspondence when she carried out her daily task of opening and sorting all the morning's mail.

Charis had posted the letter on Monday afternoon, and wasn't too disappointed when there was no reply on Wednesday because there could be a dozen reasons for its non-arrival, but when nothing arrived on either Thursday or Friday, she began to think that perhaps the officer had had other, more interesting, offers and had just thrown her letter in the waste paper basket. She spent a rather fed-up weekend, doing some decorating, plus the usual household chores, in her small one-bedroomed flat on the third floor of a converted Edwardian house overlooking Finsbury Park. She had moved into the flat about a year ago and was gradually redecorating and renovating the whole place, having got the ninety-nine-year lease at a cheaper price, because the flat needed so much doing to it. It was a task that Charis had never attempted before and she was greatly enjoying it, doing as much of the work as she could herself and only calling in the professionals when she needed something expert, like plumbing or electrical wiring, done. She made mistakes, of course, plenty of them, but found the whole experience, when she stood back and looked at what she had achieved, intensely satisfying.

The job was as good as finished now and she had intended to put the finishing touches to the last room this weekend, but disappointment made her feel gloomy and unsettled and she had to force her mind to the job. If this didn't come off, she didn't know what she was going to do; she had tried everything else, and hiring this man was a last, desperate resort. She frowned worriedly and gazed abstractedly into space, then, for the hundredth time, forced her mind back to concentrate on what she was doing.

Still half hoping for a reply, Charis went eagerly through the large pile of mail on Monday morning, but again there was nothing. On Tuesday she hardly bothered to check the envelopes, and gasped with astonishment when she picked one up addressed to J. Smith in a clear, strong handwriting. For a few moments she could only gaze at it in open-mouthed surprise and excitement, then she hastily extracted it from the other letters and stuffed it in her handbag in the bottom drawer of her desk, to read later.

The rest of the mail was got through at an incredible speed that morning; Charis whizzing into each office, dumping the post and hurrying out again without her usual cheery greeting and chat with the partners' secretaries. As soon as she could she picked up her bag and went down the corridor to the ladies' room, then fished out the envelope and opened it with nervous fingers. The letter was as brief and to the point as the advert had been: 'Dear Mr Smith, Thank you for your letter. I shall be at the Athens Bar of the Olympic Hotel at twelve-thirty on Wednesday the sixth. I shall carry a copy of the *Daily Messenger* as identification. Yours sincerely,' and then followed a longish signature of firm strokes that was almost as undecipherable as Charis' J. Smith had been. All she could make out was that it definitely started with an R and seemed to finish with an X. Which immediately made her start to worry that the man was a foreigner; after all, he hadn't said *which* army he was an officer in.

But it was the time and place that made her eyebrows go up the highest, because Wednesday, the sixth, was tomorrow, and the Olympia was one of the best hotels in London. The time she could manage easily, the hotel wasn't too far away and it was in her lunch hour, and she would be able to take extra time if she needed it because Mr Carter, the senior partner, had promised to help her in any way he could—not that anything he had been able to do so far had been of use, which was why she had been forced to take this step herself. It was the choice of hotel that worried her; if this man was used to staying at such an expensive place he might want more in payment than she could afford.

Later that morning she had a word with Mr Carter, explaining that she had to meet someone but not going into details of who or why. He looked at her sharply but didn't ask any questions merely warning her to be very careful. Charis assured him that there was no danger, nothing to worry about, then spent the whole day anxiously working out what she would say to the man and worrying about what he would be like.

That evening she washed her shoulder-length fair hair and picked out a dress and jacket to wear, then sat down and wrote out a list of all the questions she wanted to ask. It was the first time she had ever conducted an interview like this and she felt that she needed all the confidence and advantages she could get.

For that reason she arrived at the Olympic early the next day, at twelve instead of twelve-thirty. The Athens Bar was off to the right of the main reception area and, predictably, was decorated with murals showing the most touristy ancient ruins of the capital city. It was early yet and there were only a few people in there. Charis took a seat in a booth against the far wall where she could watch the doorway easily, and ordered a drink from the hovering waiter—a non-alcoholic one because she wanted to keep all her wits about her.

Sipping her drink, she looked around her; there were two fashionably dressed women with their heads close together in a nearby booth, obviously exchanging gossip, two couples having a pre-lunch cocktail, a man sitting by himself doing the crossword puzzle in the paper, and a group of four businessmen talking shop too loudly over in the corner. Gradually the place began to fill up, and at twelve-twenty Charis sat up expectantly as a tall, early middle-aged man came in alone. He stood in the doorway for a moment looking round. His eyes came to Charis, passed over her, and then he walked briskly over to the bar and greeted another man there. Disappointed, Charis settled back in her seat, then mentally kicked herself; the man hadn't been carrying a paper. Lots more people came in, and she looked them over eagerly, but none were lone men ostentatiously holding a copy of the *Daily Messenger*.

People began to drift away to lunch and Charis glanced at her watch. Nearly one o'clock. He was late, which wasn't a very good sign. The waiter came to her again and she ordered another drink, although she didn't really want it. The two couples who had been there when she came in left, and the four businessmen's voices had now grown quite raucous as they laughed and swapped dirty jokes. The other man had finished his crossword and was reading the sports pages. Charis wished she had had the presence of mind to bring something to look at, but knew she wouldn't have been able to, she was much too keyed up to read.

At one-fifteen the businessmen left and Charis gave up hope. Obviously the man must have changed his mind or else accepted another offer since he sent his letter. Miserably she looked down at her drink and wondered what to do. There didn't really seem much point in staying on here, although there was always the possibility that he'd been held up in the traffic. She decided to wait until one-thirty and then go.

She glanced hopefully round the room again, just in case someone had slipped in without her noticing. The man who had been doing the crossword looked up as she did so and caught her eye, looking at her keenly. Charis flushed slightly and quickly looked away; the last thing she wanted was for someone to try and pick her up. That was the worst of being alone in a bar; men always thought you were there for only one reason. But out of the corner of her eye she saw the man fold up his paper, finish his drink, and then get up and deliberately walk over to her. He stood in front of her, very tall and broad, shutting out the rest of the room.

Charis looked up and glared at him, daring him to speak to her.

But his mouth merely twisted in amused mockery as he said, 'Either you've been stood up by a date . . .'

She opened her mouth to indignantly deny it and tell him to go away, but he leant forward, half unfolded his paper and laid it on the table, headlines upwards.

'Or,' he went on, 'you're J. Smith.'

Charis looked at the name '*Daily Messenger*' in large letters across the newspaper, and her mouth fell open. Slowly she looked up at the man again and said rather faintly, 'But you've been here all the time.'

'That's right.' He sat down opposite her in the booth without asking permission. 'Doing the same thing that you were doing—getting here first to sum up the other party before I made contact.'

'Oh!' Completely taken aback, Caris could only stare at him speechlessly. He was younger than she had expected, about thirty-three or four, she guessed, with thick dark brown hair brushed back from his forehead. She didn't know why, but she had expected him to have a rugged, weatherbeaten appearance, but this man's face was clean-cut with a strong, square jaw and his skin was rather pale as if he had been indoors a lot. There were lines around his thin-lipped mouth that weren't laughter lines, and his left eyebrow was slightly higher than the other as if he looked on life with a certain cynicism.

The eyebrow rose now. 'You're staring,' he pointed out.

'Oh, I'm sorry.' Caris flushed and tried to pull herself together. 'How—how did you know it was me?'

'You were looking at the doorway all the time, and no one else came up to me at twelve-thirty although I was brandishing the paper. So I thought for some time that you were just late. I wasn't expecting a woman, you see.'

'No, I suppose not. I'm sorry I didn't spot the paper; I just didn't think it could be you because you were here so early.'

'It would have saved quite some time if you had,' he pointed out dryly. 'However, now that we've found each other perhaps we could get down to business.'

'Yes. Yes, of course.' But Charis was so thrown that she couldn't think of any of her questions. 'I—er—I take it you haven't taken on any other work?'

'I've had one or two offers that I'm considering.'

'Oh.' She floundered again, feeling completely out of her depth.

The man came to her rescue. 'Perhaps you'd like me to tell you something about myself?' She nodded gratefully and he went on, 'My name's Rafe Hendrix. As I said in my advert, I was in the Army up until a short time ago and I've had several years' experience at the management level as well as doing practical fieldwork with a paratroop regiment. I'm willing to undertake most jobs as long as I find them interesting—and they're legal, of course,' he added as an afterthought, almost as if it was hardly necessary to say it because it was so unlikely that a young girl like her would want anything illegal done.

'Why did you leave the army?' Charis asked him, more to give herself time to think than because she really wanted to know.

His eyes had been shadowed up to now, but suddenly he looked at her sharply and she saw that they were a strikingly deep blue and disconcertingly alert. But his tone was mild enough as he answered, 'All the regiments in the Army are being cut back because of the recession.'

'Yes, I see.' She picked up her glass and sipped at it, trying to make up her mind whether or not to trust him. It had all seemed so easy when she saw the advert in the paper, like an answer to a prayer, but now she wasn't so sure. He seemed so self-contained and withdrawn, talking to her in a crisp, educated voice and telling her of his experience, but really revealing nothing of his true self. If anything his manner was one of sardonic amusement, mockery almost, so that she felt young and gauche, as if she ought to just apologise for wasting his time and go. But she was too desperate to let her own feelings count, she had at least to *try*. Abruptly she said, 'How much do you charge, please?'

The blue eyes settled on her again and perhaps saw some of the worry in her face and the way her hands were gripped together on the table, because his voice was milder when he said, 'That would depend on what you want me to do. Would you want me to go abroad, for example?'

'Oh, no. Or at least I don't think so.' She bit her lip, again undecided.

Rafe Hendrix leant forward and said reasonably, 'Look, if you want me to work for you then you'll have to trust me. Why don't you tell me the whole story?' A glint of real amusement came into his eyes. 'You might start by telling me your real name?'

Charis' grey eyes came up to meet his for a brief instant of understanding, but it was long enough to resolve her doubts. She would tell him and then it was up to him to decide.

She gave a wry half-smile. 'I'm afraid I'm not very good at this kind of thing, am I?'

He shrugged. 'I don't suppose you've ever done it before. Neither have I, for that matter.'

Charis looked at him quickly, but his eyes were shadowed again, his rather heavy lids giving him a slightly casual air that she realised now was very deceptive; there was nothing casual about him at all. She sat up straighter in her seat and began, 'My name is Charis Radcliffe. I want you to help me find someone and then to,' she took a deep breath, 'and then to kidnap her.'

His head came up at that, his eyes resting on her instantly. 'Her?'

'Yes. My sister Jane. She's younger than me, only just nineteen.' Charis' voice broke a little and her hands tightened until the knuckles showed white. 'She's at university—or at least she was—but she took a holiday job at a hotel down in Cornwall during the Easter vacation, and while she was there she got friendly with some other young people who introduced her to a religious sect calling themselves the New Brotherhood. Instead of going back to the university she went with them to their headquarters in Bristol and, apart from one letter telling me what she was going to do, I haven't heard from her since.'

'Have you tried to contact her?'

'Yes, I've written loads of times and I've been down to Bristol twice to try and find her, but the people on the door wouldn't let me in. They said it was a holy place,' Charis added bitterly, 'and that the presence of an unbeliever would profane it. But it was really just a big old house on the outskirts of the town with a high wall round it.'

'What about your parents, have they tried to see her?'

'We haven't any parents,' Charis answered simply. 'They were killed in a car accident nearly ten years ago. But I did have a solicitor go down to Bristol and he managed to insist on seeing Jane.' She paused and a disconsolate look came into her eyes. 'But Jane refused to leave with him; she said she was happy there and wanted to devote her life to the New Brotherhood.'

'Is she religiously minded?'

'Oh, good heaven's, no!' Charis smiled in remembrance. 'Jane's full of life and fun. It was more in her nature to laugh at people who went to extremes like that. She's just not the type, and I'm sure she's either being kept there against her will or else she's been brainwashed so much that she's lost her own personality and will-power.'

'I see. You said that you wanted me to help you find her—isn't she at the place in Bristol any more, then?'

'No. Mr Carter—that's our solicitor—went there a second time to try and get Jane to sign some papers about her investments, and perhaps to talk to her again and get her to sign a document giving him the power to take her away. But the man in charge there, who calls himself the Reverend Baxter, said that she'd left and gone to live at one of their communes in the country. He wouldn't say which one, of course, and we haven't been able to find out, although Mr Carter has written several times and I went down to Bristol again and tried to find out by talking to some of the converts.'

'But you didn't actually go inside the headquarters?'

Charis shook her head regretfully. 'No, but I hung around outside until some of the younger people came out and I tried to talk to them, but they must have been warned, because when I said who I was they wouldn't talk to me.'

'Hmn, quite a problem.' Rafe Hendrix sat back and looked at her. 'You mentioned some investments; does that mean your sister has money?'

'Yes.' Charis sighed unhappily. 'When our parents died our house was sold and the money invested for us. We were to get half each when we reached the age of twenty-one. I think this is one of the main reasons why the Brotherhood won't let us see her, they're determined to keep her in the sect until she comes into her money and then make her give it to them. Everyone who joins has to hand over all their property to the sect, you see.'

'Is it a lot of money?'

'About fifty thousand pounds.'

'Yes, I can see why they want to hang on to her. Have they got many communes?'

'Four that we know about.'

He looked thoughtful for a minute and then said, 'You say that you want me to help you kidnap your sister; are you sure that there's no other way?'

'I've tried everything,' Charis told him on a note of despair. 'I even asked Mr Carter to have her made a Ward of Court, but she's over eighteen and as that's the legal age limit there's nothing we can do. Especially as she told him she was there of her own free will.' She bit her lip and said, 'I know you're thinking that kidnapping is a crime, even if it's your own sister, but I'm desperate, Mr Hendrix. I can't think of any other way. Oh, I know in your advert you said you would only consider something that was legal, but I can't get Jane out by myself and I didn't know how to contact someone who was prepared to do something that wasn't legal.' She gave a ghost of a smile. 'They don't seem to advertise themselves very much. Of course,' she went on stiltedly, 'I shall quite understand if you feel unable to help me, but if you will, then I'm—I'm able to pay you adequately for your—your assistance.'

Rafe Hendrix's mouth twisted sardonically. 'You mean you're prepared to bribe me to break the law?'

Charis winced at his bluntness but replied baldly, 'Yes, exactly that.'

'Out of your half of your parents' estate?'

'Yes.' She looked at him in some puzzlement at the question.

'You must love your sister a lot?'

'She's all I have. We've always been close, especially since our parents died. I've always looked after her, you see.'

'Yes, I understand that you feel responsible.' He leant back against the wall of the booth, apparently lost in thought, while Charis wondered anxiously what he was thinking. Under the cover of the table she crossed her fingers hopefully.

'You realise,' he said after a few moments, 'that I couldn't do this alone? I'd have to have help.'

'I'd help you,' Charis answered immediately.

His eyes settled on her appraisingly. 'You?'

'Yes.'

'You wouldn't be afraid?'

She looked at him steadily. 'Probably. But I want to get my sister out.'

The waiter came up and asked them if they'd like a last drink. Charis shook her head, but then realised that she ought really to have asked the major earlier if he would like one. 'Er—perhaps you'd like a drink?' she asked diffidently.

He shook his head decisively, the gesture in itself a dismissal to the waiter. Then he sat forward again. 'Are you quite sure you've thought this thing out? What if your sister refuses to come with us?'

Charis liked the sound of the 'us', it sounded hopeful. 'I've thought of very little else ever since I read about some people who'd been forced to do the same thing; they kidnapped their daughter from a sect in America,' she explained, adding, 'I'm pretty sure that she won't come with us willingly, we would have to use force.'

'What sort of force?'

'Well, nothing violent, of course. I thought we could make her unconscious by using chloroform, or else we could put a sack over her head or something.'

Again a flash of genuine amusement lit his blue eyes, but he agreed gravely, 'Yes, that sounds reasonable. And what if we're successful and get her out? Have you thought about where you're going to take her?

She'll very likely try and get back to them, you know,'
he pointed out steadily.

'Yes, I know. But that's all taken care of. Mr Carter
knows of a private nursing home where she can stay
and receive treatment from a psychiatrist—de-pro-
gramming, they call it.'

His left eyebrow raised in surprise, Rafe Hendrix
said, 'You've discussed this with your solicitor?'

'About kidnapping Jane?' Charis shook her head.
'No, I couldn't. He wouldn't have anything to do with
something that was illegal. No, we just made prepara-
tions in case he managed to persuade Jane to leave. I
was afraid to take her to my flat, because I'm sure the
Brotherhood know my address from the letters that
I've written to Jane, and they might have tried to get
her back, so we thought the nursing home was a good
place to take her.' She hesitated, then added unhappily,
'Sometimes they have patients there who are mentally
ill and they have some rooms with bars at the windows
so people can't get out. I thought that if I managed to
get Jane out she could be locked in one of those rooms
until she was better. I read that it can take several
weeks, depending on how long the victims have been
indoctrinated.'

'And Jane has been in there how long—since Easter,
you said, didn't you?'

'Yes, three months.'

'Then obviously the sooner you get her out the
better.'

'Yes.' Charis couldn't think of anything else to say,
of any other arguments that might persuade him to
help her. He said he had had other offers, might even
have had other answers to his advert that he hadn't yet

had time to follow up, and so might make her wait for an answer. But patience wasn't one of Charis' strong points and she said, 'Do you think, Major Hendrix, that you'll . . .'

He stood up abruptly. 'Let's go, shall we?' and he moved out of the booth.

More than a little startled, Charis hastily picked up her bag. He waited for her and then walked briskly out of the hotel.

'There's a park just down here,' he told her, gesturing to his left, and turned towards it without waiting for her to say whether she wanted to go.

By the time they reached it Charis had realised that he was walking with a limp, favouring his left leg. They turned through the open wrought-iron gates of the park and walked silently along one of the tree-lined paths. It was almost the end of June and the trees were in full leaf now, rippling in the slight wind that stopped the day from being really warm.

They had walked for several hundred yards before Rafe Hendrix said curtly, 'I expect you're wondering about the limp. You shouldn't be afraid to ask questions, you know, if you're thinking of employing someone.' He paused, but Charis didn't say anything, so he went on, his voice harsh but unemotional, 'I was injured in an . . .' there was the slightest hesitation, 'an accident at the beginning of the year. It's left me with this limp, but apart from that I'm perfectly fit. At the moment it slows me down a little when I'm running, but I'm working on that.'

Charis could imagine that he would be; somehow she thought that this wasn't the kind of man who would ever be able to tolerate having even such a small handicap if he could possibly avoid it. And his accident explained several things: why he was free to take on a job until he was fit enough, by army standards, to rejoin his unit, his pallor from having been in hospital, and the lines round his mouth.

He stopped and turned to look at her. 'Are you still willing to take me on?'

'Yes.' The reply was given instantly, without a second's hesitation for thought.

He looked at her with surprised intentness for a moment. 'Don't you want to go home and think about it?'

'No.'

He grinned suddenly and lost that grim look from his eyes and around his mouth. 'Don't you think I ought to tell you first how much I want?'

She flushed in confusion. 'Oh, yes, of course.'

'Would two hundred and fifty pounds a week, plus expenses, be all right?'

Charis gave an inner gasp of relief; it was a lot, but only about half of what she had expected to have to pay someone to help her do something illegal. She gave him a radiant smile. 'Yes. Oh, yes, that's fine.'

'Okay, you've got a deal.' He grinned again and held out his hand. 'Let's shake on it.'

Charis grasped his hand and shook it. His clasp was very strong and firm. 'Thank you, Major. When shall we . . .'

The hand in hers jerked and he said harshly, 'Don't call me that!'

Charis' eager smile left her face and she quickly took her hand away. 'I—I'm sorry.'

She turned as if to walk on, but he put out a hand to

stop her. 'No—please. It's just that I'm no longer in the Army, and I'm not one of the kind of men who like to carry an obsolete title through the rest of their life with them.'

'You're not going back in the Army when your leg is completely better?' Charis asked tentatively, realising that it was a sore subject.

'No,' he told her, his voice grim again, 'I've been invalided out.'

Charis didn't know what to say, and felt that any remark, any expression of sympathy, would be completely wrong. He had turned away, begun to walk on. Catching him up, Charis said in as businesslike tone as she could manage, 'Well, now that you've taken on the job, when can you start?'

He glanced at her and the grim look gave way to mockery again. 'We'll have to work out a plan of campaign first.' The phrase itself was a hackneyed cliché but coming from him, from an ex-soldier, it didn't sound at all incongruous. 'I'm going to need your help, you know. Do you go out to work? Can you get time off?'

'Oh, yes. That's all taken care of,' Charis replied promptly. 'My boss knows about Jane and has been very good about it. He'll let me have all the time off that I need.' That her boss, Mr Carter, was also their solicitor and had been named as a trustee in their parents' wills she didn't bother to go into.

'All right, but first I think I'd like to do some homework and find out all I can about the sect. Do you know much about them? Who runs it, how many members they have, that sort of thing?'

'I found out everything I could, but unfortunately it

isn't very much,' Charis answered ruefully. 'They try to keep a low profile and avoid publicity as much as possible. The first I ever heard of them was when Jane wrote to me and told me she was joining them. She wanted me to join, too, so she told me quite a few things about them—the good things, of course. The only other information I got on them was from a book I ordered from the library about *all* the new religious sects.'

'So she asked you to join her, did she? The head of the sect probably told her to because he found out that you had some money too. That could be useful.'

Charis looked at him with some misgivings. 'Could it?'

Again that quick glance and look of mocking amusement. 'Don't worry, I won't let you get hooked as well.'

They had walked the full circle of the little park and were back at the wrought-iron gates. They came to a mutual stop and Charis looked at him expectantly, quite confident that he would know what to do.

'Look, give me a couple of days to find out what I can. I've one or two contacts who might be able to give me more information about the sect than is known to the general public. Can you meet me on Saturday?'

'Yes, of course. Where? At the Olympia again?'

'How about here?' He indicated a nearby park bench with a nod of his head. 'At eleven?'

'That's fine. You're not staying at the Olympia, then?'

He gave a brisk, negative shake of his head. 'No, at my club, about three minutes walk away. The Olympia is above my touch.'

'But was useful to impress anyone who might want to employ you,' Charis remarked shrewdly.

His eyes settled on her face. 'Quite so.'

She hesitated, then said, 'Mr Hendrix, the other offers you had . . .'

'Don't worry,' he said curtly. 'I won't go back on my word.'

She flushed. 'That wasn't what I meant. I'm quite sure you won't. I just wondered why you accepted my offer instead of theirs.'

'Oh,' he answered with sardonic flippancy, 'I never could resist a lady in distress.'

Charis somehow found that remark denigrating. She looked down at the ground for a moment, then lifted her head and said coolly, 'Well, goodbye, Mr Hendrix. I'll see you here on Saturday at eleven.' She didn't offer to shake hands with him again but merely gave a brief nod, then turned and walked away down the street towards the tube station.

After she had gone twenty yards or so her footsteps slowed and she glanced back over her shoulder. The man whose services she had hired was limping briskly along in the opposite direction. He didn't look back.

CHAPTER TWO

WHEN Charis got up early on Saturday morning, she pushed open her bedroom window and saw that there was a ground mist hanging over the green acres of the park. She breathed deeply, enjoying the smell of the untainted, dew-laden air before it became polluted by carbon monoxide fumes from all the traffic fighting its way to and from central London. If she closed her eyes she could listen to the birds' song and almost imagine she was deep in the country somewhere. She loved the country, had always done so ever since she was a little girl and had gone there for holidays with her parents, who had often talked of moving out of London as soon as they could afford it. But the holidays had come to an abrupt end when her parents were killed, and the idea of living in the country an impossible dream that was nurtured only in the more pleasant moments of a not very happy childhood. For a while, when her schooldays were almost over, she had again thought about the possibility of getting a job somewhere in the country, but Jane was still at school in London and then Mr Carter had kindly offered her the job in his firm, and there had been no choice but to accept gratefully. A decent job, even in London, for someone with not very good academic qualifications was hard to find nowadays, and Caris knew that she was lucky to get it and must hold on to it. So she had searched until she had found this flat in North London overlooking a park, realising that this was as near as she was ever likely to get to the real country, and had bought the ninety-nine-year lease which had taken the larger part of the money her parents had left her, leaving her with enough over to furnish the flat and five thousand pounds that she had put by for a rainy day.

Only she hadn't expected the rainy day to come along quite so quickly.

Charis sighed and stepped back into the room. Methodically she made breakfast and then tidied and cleaned the flat before showering and getting ready to go out. By that time the morning mist had lifted and sun was pouring through the windows. She dressed with care, putting on a neat, pale blue sleeveless dress with a full skirt. Her ash-blonde hair fell straight and shining to her shoulders, well-cut and clean-smelling but far from the highly permed and way-out hairstyles that were fashionable among her London contemporaries. As a matter of fact she didn't go in for the changing fashions very much at all, preferring neat and simple clothes that flattered her tall, rather too slim, figure without being obtrusive. Going to the mirror, she put on a modicum of make-up: some foundation, a touch of eyebrow pencil to emphasise her straight brows, some powder on her nose and a pale pink lipstick. Sometimes, if she was going out somewhere very special, she would add eye-shadow and mascara, but her lashes and brows were naturally dark—a contrast to her fair hair—and didn't really need it.

But today she looked at herself critically in the mirror, wondering whether to add the other cosmetics. Her bone structure was good, with high cheekbones, a wide forehead and small, straight nose. Her eyes, of a pale grey, were set wide apart, giving her a level, rather grave look. Usually her eyes were serene and untroubled, but the weeks of worry about Jane had left shadows around them that weren't unattractive. Not that Charis considered herself to be attractive; she was okay, not dead plain or anything, but she seemed quite dull in comparison with Jane who had shining good looks which, added to her natural vivacity, made her beautiful. Wherever Jane went she was popular, gathering friends and admirers, always the centre of any circle, never without companionship. And Charis had been content that it should be so, recognising the basic differences in their characters and not wanting to make any changes, happy in her sister's popularity and beauty and as proud of her as any parent.

Charis sighed again, wretchedly, as she wondered where her sister was now and what was happening to her, then brightened as she remembered her meeting with Rafe Hendrix this morning. She picked up her handbag and checked its contents before letting herself out of the flat. At least she was trying to do something positive, and had some hope for the future.

She made her way briskly through the throng of Saturday morning shoppers, flashed her season ticket to the man on duty at Finsbury Park Underground station, walked along the echoing brick tunnels to the platform, and was soon on a tube train to the West End. There was only a short distance to walk at the other end and she was a few minutes early, but not at all surprised to see Rafe Hendrix there before her, seated on the park bench with a businesslike-looking briefcase on the floor at his feet.

He got to his feet as she approached. 'Good morning.'

Charis smiled at him warmly. 'Good morning, Mr Hendrix,' adding eagerly, 'Did you manage to find out anything?'

'One or two things that might be interesting.' He gestured to the bench and Charis sat down beside him. His eyes went over her, as if reaffirming his first impressions, then, surprising her, he said, 'Look, if we're going to be partners in crime, as it were, don't you think that it might make it easier if we're on first name terms? Mine's Rafe, if you remember.'

After a second's hesitation, she said, 'Mine's Charis.'

'Yes, I know. It's very unusual.'

He stooped, then, to pick up his briefcase and open it, sort out the papers inside, giving Charis time to look at him. He had been wearing a dark business suit the first time they had met, but this time he was wearing more casual tan cavalry twill slacks, a cream shirt open at the neck and a brown jacket. The more casual clothes, however, didn't make him any less intimidating.

Rafe opened a notebook and said, 'One of my contacts works for a national newspaper and he managed to give me a few details, but not much more than you already know, I'm afraid. It seems that the sect's full title is The New Brotherhood for Hope and Peace in the World. Quite a mouthful! It's actually a splinter group off another splinter group from a really well-known sect that originated in the Far East and is now world-wide. The New Brotherhood, however, seems to operate only in this country, there's nothing about them trying to spread abroad. As you said, they keep a very low profile generally, but there have been one or two incidents that have made news, although there was nothing startling. Twice parents have gone to one of their camps or communes trying to get their children back and the police have been called in.'

'Were they successful?' Charis broke in.

He shook his head curtly. 'No, afraid not. In both cases the parents were eventually allowed to confront their children in the presence of a police officer, but both the children refused to leave, so there was nothing they could do.' He paused, turned a page and went on, 'They once had a commune on a farm near Cirencester, but they made the mistake of trying to recruit youngsters from the neighbouring area, and the locals cut up so rough that it made it impossible for them to carry on there and they had to sell up and move out.'

'Good for them,' said Charis with feeling. 'I wish the people near their other communes would do the same thing.'

'Not much chance, I'm afraid. That happened several years ago and they seemed to have learnt their lesson. Now they confine their recruiting to holiday resorts and big towns where they're likely to find young people away from their parents' protection.'

'Has anyone ever got away from them?' Charis asked him rather forlornly.

'A few. The local people I told you about near Cirencester got together and went to the camp en masse and were able to forcibly take their children back before they'd become too deeply involved.'

'What else did you find out?'

'That there are only four communes other than their headquarters in Bristol. They're all in the West

Country area: one in between Chippenham and Calne
in Wiltshire, two up towards Gloucester, and one in
the Wye Valley near Ledbury. They don't seem to send
people direct from Bristol to any particular commune,
so Jane could be at any one of them. We'll have to
investigate them all one by one.'

'How do we do that?'

Rafe gave a slightly crooked grin. 'I expect we'll
think of something.'

He shut the notebook and Charis said in disappointment and some surprise, 'Is that all you found out?'
She had expected him to go on, because she had
glimpsed several pages of the notebook filled with his
handwriting.

'Nothing of any interest.' He went to slip the notebook into the inside pocket of his jacket, but he had
hesitated for a fraction of a second before answering,
so Charis put out a hand to stop him.

'No—wait! You said we were going to be partners,
so don't you think you ought to tell me everything you
found out?'

He looked down at her hand, determinedly gripping
his sleeve, and then up at her face. 'How old are you,
Charis?' he asked gently.

She flushed a little. 'What's that got to do with it?'

'Everything.'

Her face tightened, but she answered stiffly, 'I'm
twenty-two. And I'm quite old enough to be able to
take anything—unpleasant that you might have to tell
me. So please stop treating me like a child.'

Rafe continued to look at her set face for a few
moments longer, then nodded. 'All right.' He took the
notebook out again and flipped it open. 'The other in-

formation I got was about the sect's methods of—shall we call it conversion?—for new recruits. As you said, they're not very pleasant.'

Charis' face had paled, but she said firmly, 'Tell me.'

'Okay. Well, the sect's object is to control the mind, but not to let the recruit be aware of what's happening to him, so they keep them in virtual isolation for a while and deprive them of sleep, often letting them have only about three hours a night. After a week or so of that they're like zombies and are receptive to the mass ceremonies where the leaders continually preach their doctrine. There's also constant singing in which the recruits are made to join, and they eventually get into a trancelike state in which their minds are open to brainwashing. They also pressurise the new people into throwing up their university careers and rejecting their families. They tell them that academic qualifications only lead to materialism, and they don't need their own families because the Brotherhood provides a perfect one. Nothing violent or cruel, you understand, but very effective, especially in the long term.'

'That's rather what I expected,' Charis said steadily. She looked up at him with a slight frown. 'I don't understand what you mean by providing a perfect family, though. Did you mean that they should look on the sect as their family?'

'Partly that.' Rafe paused and then seemed to make up his mind. 'But they also encourage small family units within the sect. When they've been indoctrinated, the leaders provide mates for the new recruits—they don't have any choice in the matter—and they are expected to breed a new generation of followers.'

'Oh!' Charis' face reddened with embarrassment, then she raised large, frightened eyes to meet his. 'Do you think that's happened to Jane?'

'Shouldn't think so. She hasn't been in there long enough. But I think the sooner we get her out the better.'

'So do I,' Charis agreed fervently. 'When shall we start?'

Again that crooked grin. 'We'd better work out exactly what we're going to do first.' Closing the note-book, he said, 'We'll need a photograph of Jane. A good one, so that I'll be able to recognise her easily, and preferably in colour.'

'That's easy, I've got lots of photographs of her at home.'

'Good.' He bent to the briefcase again and pulled out a map, opening it out on his knees. 'I got this map of the area we want and I've circled the sites of the four communes—the two near Gloucester, here near Chippenham, and here further north in the Wye Valley.' He pointed with a long forefinger. 'I think it would be easier if we started with the two near Gloucester, so I suggest we make our headquarters in or near the town and drive out to the communes. Do you have a car?' he asked.

Charis shook her head. 'No, I'm afraid not.'

'And you don't drive?'

'No. There's never seemed much point in learning when you live in London.'

'I suppose not.' He frowned. 'It would have helped if you could, though.' He thought for a moment, then asked, 'Does Jane have a boy-friend?'

'Not a steady one, if that's what you mean. I think

she went out a few times with one or two of the students at university, but I haven't met any of them and I don't know their names.'

'How about you? Do you have a boy-friend who'd be willing to help you?'

Charis looked down at her hands in her lap and shook her head. 'No, I haven't,' she said flatly.

He didn't pursue it, just accepted her statement. 'In that case you'd better send off for a provisional licence immediately and I'll give you a crash course while we're in Gloucestershire. Your solicitors will send it on to you, won't they?'

'Yes.' She looked at him uncertainly. 'Do you have a car?'

'No, but I can get one.'

'And can you—er——' she fumbled, 'are you able to drive?'

'Because of my leg, d'you mean? Yes, of course I can drive,' he answered shortly. 'But circumstances might arise where I had my hands full and it would help if you could handle a car.'

'Yes, I see. I'll send off for one straightaway.' Charis had no need to ask Rafe what he meant by having his hands full; if Jane refused to go with them voluntarily, she could quite easily envisage him having to hold her down.

Rafe folded the map. 'Did many of the people at the headquarters in Bristol see you when you went down there? Do you think they might recognise you again?'

'I suppose I must have spoken to about twenty people,' Charis told him, trying to remember. 'They might remember me.'

'How long ago was it?'

'About six weeks.'

He looked at her appraisingly. 'Are you and your sister very much alike?'

Charis smiled and shook her head. 'Not really. We're about the same height and build and our colouring is similar, but Jane is more of a honey blonde and she's very pretty. She's the beauty of the family,' she added with another smile.

'Is she? You surprise me.'

The dry tone in which he said it made Charis look up at him swiftly, but he had taken an engagement diary from his case and was flicking the pages. 'There are a few things I want to get that I think might come in useful, and, of course, I have to get hold of a car, but I think I'll have everything together by Tuesday. How about you? Could you be ready to leave for Gloucester first thing Wednesday morning?'

Her breath caught in her throat for a moment, then she said hastily, 'Yes. Yes, of course I could. Any time you say.'

He looked at her narrowly. 'You're quite sure you want to go through with this?'

'Yes, I'm quite sure.' Her grey eyes looked steadily into his. 'Is there anything you want me to bring?'

'Some form of identification to prove who you are, that Jane is your sister and that you're her next of kin might help. Just in case.'

Charis didn't have to ask what 'just in case' meant; the very thought made her go cold. 'Yes, all right. Anything else?'

'Some tough outdoor clothes: denim jeans and an anorak, that kind of thing. Oh, and a pair of rubber boots. We might have to pretend to be hikers out for a walk or something. You'd better bring enough things to last for a few weeks; there's no knowing how long it's going to take. But apart from that I can't think of anything.'

'What time on Wednesday?'

'I'd like to make as early a start as possible. Where do you live?' Charis told him and he said, 'Then I'll call for you at six in the morning.'

'But wouldn't it be out of your way?' Charis objected. 'I could come up to the West End on the train and meet you somewhere, if you like?'

His blue eyes settled on her face. 'You'd lug your suitcases all the way up to town just to save me coming out of my way?'

'I don't mind,' Charis told him diffidently.

'Well, you should mind. You should have a sense of your own importance,' he told her forcefully. Charis was too taken aback by his tone to speak, so he snapped his briefcase shut and stood up. 'I'll pick you up on Wednesday.'

'Yes, all right.' Charis too got to her feet and said uncertainly, 'Would you like some money now for the things you said you wanted to get? I'm afraid I'd have to give you a cheque, though. Oh, and do I pay you in advance or at the end of every week?'

She looked up at him and was startled to see a flash of anger in Rafe's eyes and she was afraid that she had offended him, but he merely said, 'Suppose I send you a bill for everything when the job's finished?'

A doubtful look came into her face. 'Are you sure? I don't want you to be out of pocket.'

'Quite sure,' he told her firmly. 'Now, is there anything else you want to ask me?'

Charis slowly shook her head. 'I don't think so—oh, unless you want me to get some chloroform?'

For the first time that day, amusement shone in his eyes. 'You're very determined on that, aren't you? But I think we'll wait until we've found out a little more first. Besides, it might be a little awkward to get hold of; you might have to sign for it in the chemist's or something, which we don't really want.'

A slightly wistful look crossed Charis' face, but then she shrugged and laughed. 'Yes, I suppose it could be awkward.'

Rafe smiled back at her. 'You've obviously been reading too many old detective stories,' he said lightly.

'Don't they use chloroform in modern ones, then?'

'No, they seem to resort to more violent methods,' he answered drily. Lifting his head, he looked up at the sky for a moment, watching two birds that quarrelled loudly as they flew among the trees. Charis wondered if their meeting was over and she ought to take her leave, but just as she made a move to speak, he looked at her again and said, 'Let's take a turn around the park.'

Charis fell into step beside him and they began to walk down the flower-bordered shingle path. There weren't many people in the park today; all the commuters were at home and there was only an elderly man walking his dog, a woman pushing a toddler in a pushchair, and a young couple strolling hand in hand, their heads close together, lost to everything else but their own company, the happiness of being together.

'Tell me about your sister,' said Rafe, cutting into her thoughts.

'What do you want to know?'

'Everything. Everything you can tell me about her.'

'Well,' Charis tried to gather the information into some sort of order, 'as I said, she's just nineteen. She's a very bright and happy person. Quite clever; she got seven O-levels and three A-level passes at school. She likes games, especially tennis. Oh, and she loves going to the theatre, always has ever since she was a little girl. She always used to choose an outing to the theatre as her birthday treat when our parents were alive, but afterwards we had to save our pocket money up until we had enough for a seat in the gods.'

'Who looked after you when your parents died?'

Charis fixed her eyes on a bed of deep red roses and wasn't aware that Rafe was watching her and had noted the rather grim, set look that came to her face. 'First of all we were sent to live with our paternal grandparents, but then they got a divorce and we were sent away to school. In the holidays we went to children's camps in the summer, and to a distant cousin's at Christmas and Easter. He was a clergyman attached to a very high church and we used to spend most of the holidays at church services, which is why I couldn't believe that Jane would get mixed up with a religious cult; we used to get so bored.'

'Maybe because it's a different kind of religion?'

'Perhaps,' Charis agreed doubtfully. 'But I just can't see it.'

They walked on for a little way in silence, beneath the shadows of the trees and then out into bright sunlight again.

'It doesn't sound as if you had a very happy childhood,' Rafe remarked.

Charis shrugged. 'It was just that both our parents

were only children and we had very few relations. The ones we did have were quite elderly and either didn't want young children around or didn't know what to do with us. But please don't think that people were unkind; we were always well looked after and didn't go short of anything. And we always had each other, we were never separated.' Her face glowed. 'And I remember once we had the most wonderful summer; some friends of Mummy and Daddy took us away with their family and we spent the whole of the school holidays camping in France. That was a simply marvellous time.' The glow faded and her face grew sombre again. 'They told me later that Mummy and Daddy had wanted them to be our legal guardians, but they'd never got round to making a will. They did try to adopt us, but Grandfather wouldn't allow it. I expect he thought they were only doing it because of our money.'

Charis paused, then said, 'I think it's a great mistake not to make a will, don't you? People always think that nothing will happen to them, that it only happens to other people, which is silly. I made my will the minute I was eighteen. Have you made one?' she asked, turning to look at him.

'You have to when you join the Army.'

'Oh, yes, of course. Not that there's much danger of being killed in peacetime, is there?'

'Can't you talk about something more pleasant?' he grated with sudden harshness. 'You were telling me about your sister.'

His sudden change took her aback and she stammered a little as she said, 'I'm sorry. There's not much more to tell about Jane really. She was reading history at university, but she wasn't sure what she wanted to do when she left. She loves animals, and she has lots of toy ones on her bed at home. She doesn't like being alone in the dark. Her favourite colour is pink.' Charis stopped abruptly, aware that she was just picking facts out of the air and was making no sense. 'Is there anything else you want to know?' she asked stiltedly.

'Not at the moment.' They walked in silence for the few minutes it took to circle the park and then Rafe glanced at his watch. 'It's rather early, but how about having lunch?'

Charis was on the point of saying yes, but hesitated, seeing the brooding look about his mouth and remembering the curt way he had cut her off. 'Thanks, but if we're leaving on Wednesday I've a lot to do.'

His eyebrows flickered but he only said, 'As you wish. I'll pick you up at six on Wednesday, then. Can I get in touch with you quickly through your solicitors if anything crops up?'

'Yes, they'll pass on a message immediately.'

'Till Wednesday, then.' He lifted a hand in a half salute and turned away.

Charis turned in the other direction and this time didn't look after him. It was true that she had a lot to do before Wednesday, but she didn't hurry home straightaway. Instead she made her way down to the Embankment and sat on a seat facing the river. The tide was out and birds wheeled above the exposed mud flats. Two teenagers waded along at the water's edge with metal detectors and farther along a dog was worrying a stick that was poking half out of the mud. Her eyes took in the scene, but she didn't really see it; her thoughts were too full of Rafe, the man she had

hired and whose company she would be in for an inde-
finite period. Only it didn't feel as if he was her em-
ployee, the other way round rather. Not that Charis
minded; he was so obviously used to taking charge and
planning things that she was quite happy to hand
everything over to him. Right from the first she had
been confident of his ability, and, after that first brief
hesitation, she had had no doubts about trusting him
either.

But she couldn't be completely at ease with him.
She pondered the problem, wondering if his occasional
shortness was because he was impatient with her
naïvety. Why else had he asked her how old she was?
Presumably there was a gap of over ten years between
them, and in some ways, she knew, she was young for
her age. She had no worldly experience, as Rafe must
have, hadn't travelled very much or spent years in
pursuit of a career. All she'd had was school, Mr
Carter's office and looking after Jane, she thought
ruefully. But she did have fortitude and a quiet sort of
courage that had carried her through some difficult
times and in some ways made her older than her
twenty-two years. So perhaps it wasn't the age gap
after all. Perhaps it was something in Rafe himself.

Charis got up and went to lean on the wall that held
back the river. The grey stone felt hot to her arms and
there were small weeds trying, not very successfully,
to grow between the crevices. She wondered what the
next few weeks would bring and whether they would
be successful. But they just *had* to be. Life would be
impossible if they failed, knowing that Jane was still
confined within the sect, her own personality and will-
power drowned beneath religious indoctrination. *They*

just had to get her out. And everything depended on Rafe. On a man who obviously had something in his past which had made him cool and withdrawn, who kept all his emotions behind a wall of reserve as thick as the one she was leaning on, the shutters coming down immediately whenever she made a remark that got too close. And so far the only slight cracks that had appeared in his wall had been the few gleams of amusement and couple of real grins that he had given her.

And the invitation to lunch? Had that been a genuine offer or just social politeness. If she had accepted would he perhaps have opened up about himself? Charis was too inexperienced to tell and wasn't even sure that she wanted to know. All she wanted right now was a reliable person to help her to find Jane. She believed that in Rafe Hendrix she had been lucky enough to find that man and that was really all that mattered. He was old enough and tough enough to solve his own problems and probably wouldn't thank her for worrying about him anyway.

No messages came from Rafe to delay their departure, so on Wednesday morning Charis got up at dawn and did the last few chores around the flat, packed the last few things in her case and quietly took it downstairs to stand ready in the hall. She had just the one case and a rucksack which she had bought at a local camping shop. Rafe had mentioned that they might have to pretend to be walkers and she thought it would come in useful. She was ready much too early, of course, standing at the window that overlooked the street, feeling strangely nervous and wondering what kind of car he had got. Never for a moment did she doubt that he would come.

At two minutes to six a blue estate car turned into the road and drew up outside. Charis turned and ran quickly down the stairs to open the front door before he had to ring the bell and wake everyone else in the house.

'Good morning. Here's my case. I've one or two other things upstairs. I won't be a minute.' She left him to stow away her suitcase and ran lightly back up to the flat to pick up her jacket, bag and the rucksack. One last look round in case she'd forgotten anything, although she knew that she hadn't, then she closed the door and went downstairs again, pulling the front door gently shut behind her.

Rafe was standing on the pavement waiting. Today he was wearing a pair of faded denims and an old Army type sweater, the sort with patches on the shoulders and elbows that you could buy in any large department store, or off a market stall for that matter. Only those were imitations; Rafe's had marks on the shoulders where his insignia of rank had been attached and the material around them had faded.

He nodded approvingly when he saw the rucksack. 'Good thinking.' Taking it from her, he stowed it in the back and closed the rear door. Charis could see several intriguing-looking bundles and packages in there as well as a holdall and another rucksack. He opened the passenger door for her, then got in the car himself, but before starting the engine he looked at her and said, 'Did you bring the photograph and other things I asked you to get?' and when Charis nodded, he went on, 'I take it that you have told everyone who's likely to be concerned that you're going away? Your landlady and your employer, and so on? It would be rather disastrous if they thought you'd gone missing and set the police searching for you.'

'You've no need to worry,' Charis assured him. 'Everything's taken care of.'

'Good girl!' He grinned, a real grin that reached his eyes, 'Let's get going, then, shall we?'

Charis' grey eyes met his blue ones and recognised the same inner anticipation that she was feeling, an eagerness to start the search, the enterprise, call it what you will. She smiled back at him. 'Yes. Let's go, as fast as we can!'

CHAPTER THREE

THE distance from London to Gloucester is only just over a hundred miles. By starting early they avoided most of the heavy traffic on the ring road that runs round central London and had soon picked up the route that would lead them on to the M40, the motorway that heads west towards Oxford.

Rafe concentrated on his driving at first, but once they reached the motorway he seemed more disposed to talk.

'Did you send off for your provisional driving licence?'

'Yes, and I marked the application urgent, so it should be through in a few days. I told Mr Carter I'd let him know my address as soon as we were settled somewhere.'

His left eyebrow rose enquiringly. 'Mr Carter?'

'My solicitor.'

'Ah, yes. And did you also tell him what we were going to do?'

Charis smiled slightly and shook her head. 'No. I don't think he'd approve.'

'Most likely not,' Rafe agreed wryly. 'Have you told anyone else?'

'There's no one else to tell.'

They fell silent for a few miles, the road stretching on straight and wide through the green countryside, as straight as the ancient roads that the Romans had built so many centuries ago through a wilder landscape. But Charis was trying to find the words to ask a question that had been nagging her for some time; to just come right out with it would be both impolite and possibly embarrassing. At length she hedged round it by saying, 'How about you? Have you told anyone what we're going to do?'

He gave his usual curt negative gesture, and his tone was cold as he answered, 'I've respected your confidence, if that's what you're asking.'

'No, it wasn't.' She looked straight ahead through the windscreen. 'I just thought that if you were— married you would naturally have had to tell your wife where you were going.'

'What makes you think I'm married?'

Something in his tone made her look at him and she wasn't surprised to see a curl of sardonic amusement on his lips.

'I don't—nothing. I just thought you might be, that's all.' Embarrassment gave way to anger and she said tartly, 'After all, you're quite *old* enough to be married!'

He frowned and his mouth twisted more deeply. 'As you say,' he agreed, 'I'm quite old enough—but as it happens, I'm not. I've no one much to tell either.'

He bent to turn on the radio then and they both fell silent again for quite some time, Charis definitely unwilling to reopen the conversation.

After they had been driving for about two hours, Rafe pulled off the road into the forecourt of a Little Chef wayside restaurant. 'Let's go in here and have a cup of coffee, shall we?'

Charis reached into the back for her rucksack. 'As a

matter of fact I brought a flask with me in case we got thirsty on the way down. Here, I'll pour you a cup.'

'Trying to cut down on expenses?' Rafe observed mockingly, then shook his head, his expression changing and taking the sting out of the remark. 'Thanks, but I need to stretch my legs. Save it till later.'

'Oh, yes, of course. Sorry.'

He got out of the car while Charis put the rucksack back and groped for her handbag, then he came round to open her door for her and lock it behind her, a gentlemanly gesture that Charis enjoyed; she was more used to having to fight her way through the rush hour crowds in London where it was impossible to behave like a lady, let alone a gentleman. She had expected Rafe to go straight into the restaurant, but instead he turned aside and began to walk down a path alongside the car park, his limp far more pronounced than she had seen it before. She was immediately concerned.

Hurrying after him, she said anxiously, 'I didn't think you literally meant to stretch your leg. Is it very stiff? I'm sorry, I should have realised . . .'

He turned on her, his brows drawn into a frown. 'Must you damn well keep saying you're sorry?' he snapped.

Charis came to an abrupt halt and stared at him, eyes wide with surprise. She started to say, 'I'm sor . . .' then stopped. Stiffly she said, 'If you'll excuse me I think I'll wait inside,' and turned and walked back towards the restaurant without waiting for him to answer. Once inside she made straight for the ladies' loo, feeling angry and resentful and yet, at the same time, scared in case she had offended him in some way she couldn't understand. She hadn't put Rafe down as

a moody person; cynical certainly, but she had thought
that he was too self-controlled to let his emotions show.
But evidently she was wrong. Unless of course he was
having second thoughts about the whole thing and
wishing that he'd never agreed to help her. The very
idea made her go cold and for a moment panic filled
her, but then common sense came back as she remembered the light of anticipation that had shone in
Rafe's eyes when they had set off that morning. No,
whatever was troubling him it wasn't the job. So maybe
it was having to be in her company for so long. Well,
there wasn't much she could do about that except to
try not to annoy him. And as she wasn't quite sure
how she *had* annoyed him, it wasn't going to be too
easy.

When she came out of the ladies', Charis gave a
swift look round, but Rafe still hadn't come in.
Surprisingly the place was quite full, and nearly all the
customers were men; long-distance lorry drivers by the
look of them, who had stopped there for breakfast. As
she made her way to an empty table by the window,
several of them glanced up and then let their eyes linger
on her tall, slim figure. Charis took care not to look at
any of them directly, but was uncomfortably aware of
their perusal and the muttered comments they made as
she passed.

One of them, young, bearded, and bolder than the
others, put an arm out to stop her. 'Come and sit with
us, darlin'. We'll buy you some breakfast,' he offered,
gesturing to the vacant seat opposite.

'No, thank you. Please let me pass.'

She tried to push past, but he wouldn't take his arm
away, looking up at her and laughing, enjoying himself.

Behind her, Charis heard the door open and looked round rather desperately.

Rafe summed up the situation in one glance and was behind her in seconds. He fixed his eyes on the youth's face and said in a calm, almost conversational tone. 'Are you going to move your arm or do I break it?'

The grin slipped from the other's face so fast it was almost funny. Hastily he moved his arm, muttering, 'No harm done. We were only having a laugh.'

Quickly Charis moved on to the empty table and sat down. Rafe followed at a more leisurely pace and slid into the booth opposite her.

'Thank you,' Charis said feelingly.

'My fault; I should have realised and not let you come in alone.'

The waiter came up and he ordered two coffees. When it came, Charis sipped hers gratefully, enjoying its bitter flavour.

Rafe poured cream into his and stirred it thoughtfully, then looked up and said, 'I owe you an apology. I'm afraid I get rather impatient with this damn leg sometimes.'

'It's all right, it doesn't matter.'

'But it does matter,' he put in forcefully. 'I had no right to take it out on you.' He looked at her, but Charis lowered her eyes, concentrated on drinking the coffee. Ruefully he went on, 'This is the first time I've driven a car for any length of time since—the accident. It annoyed me that it had stiffened up on me. And—well, I'm sorry.'

Charis could well understand how it might; he had obviously always been so fit and healthy before that he had no time for illness or incapacity, however slight, especially his own. He would expect his body to recover immediately and be as good as before, and probably found it hard to accept that it hadn't. She looked at him as he stirred his coffee, a bleak look around his mouth, and decided that if he didn't want sympathy then he certainly wasn't going to get any. In a demure tone she said, 'You really don't have to keep apologising.'

His hand stilled and he shot a quick speculative glance across at her, saw the laughter in her eyes which immediately drew an answering gleam in his own.

'Touché. So you've a sense of humour, have you?'

She looked surprised. 'Didn't you think I had?'

He smiled slightly. 'It seems that there's quite a lot I don't know about you.'

'Or I you,' Charis returned evenly.

Rafe gave her another quick glance, and this time laughed openly when he saw the mischievous look on her face. 'Well, we'll probably have plenty of time to rectify that.'

The second half of their journey was much more enjoyable than the first. Rafe seemed far more relaxed and drew her out to talk about herself, listening as she told him about her childhood, occasionally giving her a keen glance whenever he detected a change of tone as she lightly glossed over the unhappy years.

'What about you?' she asked him. 'Where are you from?'

'Not from anywhere, really,' he answered with a slight shrug. 'My father was in the Army, you see, and although I was actually born in England, I lived with my parents wherever my father happened to be stationed: Aden, Germany, Cyprus, all over the place.

Then, when I was old enough, I came back here to school and went straight on to Sandhurst for officer training.'

'You decided to follow in your father's footsteps?'

'I didn't have to take any decision,' he replied, his mouth thinning sardonically. 'We've always been an Army family, right back to the year dot; from the moment I was born I knew that I was to be a soldier.'

'Didn't you mind?' Charis asked curiously. 'Having it all mapped out for you like that?'

He turned his head to look at her for a moment, then turned back to watch the road. 'No, strangely enough I didn't. I've always loved the Army, you see, and everything about it.'

Charis did see, more than he realised. Especially his annoyance with the bad leg that had forced him to give up a career he loved. She would have liked to have asked him more about it, but wisely forbore, realising what a sensitive subject it was. Instead she talked of other, impartial things and found him an amusing and intelligent companion so that the time and the miles just flew by.

Twice more they stopped so that Rafe could take a walk and unstiffen his leg. Towards the end of the journey the skin around his mouth began to look a little pale, and Charis was silently glad when, at about ten o'clock, they reached the outskirts of Gloucester and Rafe drew up outside a smallish but modern hotel on the main road into the town.

'This looks a likely place,' he remarked, running his eyes over it. 'Not too near the centre of town to be full of tourists. Probably patronised by commercial travellers who only stay for a day or so and then move on.'

He climbed stiffly out of the car and bent to rub his knee, grimacing a little. But as Charis walked round to join him he straightened up and his face cleared. 'Let's go in and see if they have any rooms.'

The foyer of the hotel was small, with a reception desk on the right, a couple of not very comfortable-looking chairs, and a notice-board fixed to the wall with leaflets advertising various local entertainments drawing-pinned to it. Rafe rang the electric bell on the reception desk and a woman came through a glass-panelled door of an office behind the desk. She looked them over appraisingly, and Charis felt as if she had been completely summed up in that one glance.

The woman's eyes left her, settled on Rafe and widened a little, then she gave him a smile that was half coquettish, half obsequious, 'Good morning, sir. Can I help you?'

'We'd like two single rooms, if you have them.'

The receptionist's eyebrows rose unbelievingly. 'Two *single* rooms?'

'That's what I said,' Rafe answered evenly.

'For how long, sir?'

'A week to start with. We may want to stay longer, but our plans are unsettled at the moment.'

The woman consulted a bookings ledger. 'I'm afraid I only have one single room available at the moment. I can do a single and a double, but I'll have to charge extra for the double, of course.' She looked at Charis and then back at Rafe with a knowing smile. 'It would be much cheaper for you to take the double. We're quite broadminded here; we have to be in this day and age.'

'Really?' Rafe answered scathingly. 'We, however,

are not. We'll take the double *and* the single.'

The woman shrugged, quite unperturbed. 'Very well.' She told them what the rates were and asked them to sign the register. 'Mr Hendrix and Miss Radcliffe.' She took down two keys from a hooked board behind her. 'Which of you is going to have the double room?'

Charis started to say, 'You have it,' but Rafe over-ruled her.

'The lady will take it,' he said firmly.

They took the keys and went to get their luggage out of the car and take it up to their rooms, which were both on the second floor, quite close together. Rafe had carried her case upstairs as well as his holdall, while Charis brought the backpacks.

Setting her case down outside her door, he said, 'Half an hour to freshen up and unpack and then we'll go into the town and have some lunch. Okay?'

'Fine.'

There were twin beds in Charis' room, together with a wardrobe, chest of drawers and a chair, which was the sum total of the furniture, apart from a washbasin in the corner with a cracked mirror above it. The walls were painted a serviceable cream colour and there was a limp-looking blue curtain at the window with match-ing coverlets on the beds. It looked what it was; a place where people stayed for such a short time that only the basic necessities had to be provided. Charis grimaced a little, then shrugged; it was cheap even if it wasn't very cheerful, and no one was likely to ask them any ques-tions about their comings and goings, which was all that really mattered.

When Rafe knocked on her door she was ready, her

clothes neatly put away, her face washed and re-made-up and her hair combed. His eyebrows rose when she opened the door and stepped out to join him. 'Don't tell me you're ready?'

'You said half an hour,' Charis pointed out in some surprise.

'I know. But I've never met a female yet who could be ready on time.'

She laughed. 'Well, now you have. I don't like being late.'

He shook his head unbelievingly. 'Wonders will never cease!'

They drove into the town and Rafe bought a large-scale map of the area before they found a restaurant and had lunch. Afterwards he spread the map out on the table and circled the two places where the Brotherhood had their communes near the town.

For a while during the meal, Charis had almost forgotten why they were there, but now her face sobered as she looked at the map and wondered where her sister was. 'Which one shall we go to first?' she asked.

'I think it would be best if we drove out and had a look at both places, see which one would be the easiest to watch.'

Charis looked up at him quickly. 'You mean—go now?'

'It seems as good a time as any, don't you think?'

'Yes, of course.' She stood up and was ashamed to find that her heart was beating fast and she was trembling a little now that the actual moment of looking for Jane had come.

Rafe folded the map and got to his feet. Putting a hand under her elbow, he leaned closer and said softly,

'Don't expect miracles, Charis, it might take us quite a while to locate her.'

Her eyes met his and she nodded, her heart returning to its normal beat. 'No, I won't.'

They found the first place very easily; it was a quite large farm set in the fold of the hills and visible from the minor road that went past the lane that led down to it. Rafe parked the car further along and he took out a pair of binoculars to get a closer look.

'I can see several people out working in the fields,' he told her, 'but there's a high wall round the farm itself. To see inside the wall we would have to get up higher.' He looked round and pointed off to the left. 'See that hill over there? If we climbed to the top of it we should be able to get a good view through the binoculars of anyone moving about in the farmyard. And there are quite a few trees and bushes which would conceal us from anyone looking up there.'

'Shall we go up there now?' Charis asked eagerly.

Rafe shook his head. 'No, we'll go and recce the other place first.'

The second commune was about twenty miles away, towards the southern side of Gloucester near the old Roman road called Ermin Way, but couldn't be seen from the main road, so they parked the car in a layby and walked down the narrow lane that led to it.

'This doesn't look so good,' Rafe remarked as they walked along. 'This lane only goes to a few farms and then peters out, and the banks are too high for us to get out of sight if anything comes along.' He stopped and consulted the map again. 'Mmn, that's useful. There's a youth hostel not too far from here. With our backpacks we wouldn't look at all out of place if someone saw us walking along this lane or in the nearby fields. But I think it would be better if we got off this road now.'

He went to turn back but Charis, who was a few yards in front said, 'Wait. Look, there's a gate just round the bend. Couldn't we go as far as that?'

Rafe nodded and they walked on a few yards further. The gate wasn't the usual wooden five-barred farm type; this one was made of metal bars and set between two high brick pillars. On either side of the pillars stretched a long brick wall over six feet high, topped with barbed wire, its points looking particularly vicious. On the left-hand pillar was attached a wooden board with the words 'EARLSWOOD HALL' neatly painted on it in white letters.

'Is this it?' Charis asked.

'Yes.'

'It doesn't say anything about the Brotherhood.'

'I don't suppose they care to advertise.' Rafe moved nearer and, keeping behind one of the pillars, took a quick but searching look through the bars. 'Can't see much, I'm afraid. There are too many trees in the way.' Gently, he put his hand on the gate and pushed it experimentally, but it hardly moved. 'Locked. Probably padlocked on the other side.' He took another look and said in some surprise, 'No, it's a very efficient-looking mechanism from what I can see. Damn! A padlock I could have dealt with easily, but that one looks rather a problem. Very efficient for keeping people out.'

'Or in,' Charis pointed out dryly.

'As you say.' He straightened up. 'We'd better get away from here. I think our best bet will be to start at the other commune. It's bigger and more easily accessible.'

'But surely this place would be better,' Charis argued. 'The fact that it's so impregnable must mean that they keep the more reluctant converts here—perhaps the ones who're having second thoughts, or who aren't completely indoctrinated.'

'Perhaps they do,' Rafe agreed. 'But what makes you think that Jane might be one of them? For all we know the people who are in charge of whichever commune she's in might be so confident of her—conversion that she's quite free to come and go from the place. And we would be rather wasting our time trying to get into a difficult commune before trying the easier places first. Don't you agree?'

'Yes, I suppose so.' But Charis spoke reluctantly and turned to take another look back at the barred gate.

'Don't worry,' Rafe encouraged her. 'If we can't find her at the other commune we'll try this one next.'

'But how will we get in?'

'Oh, there's always a way in.' He grinned. 'Piece of cake!'

Charis looked at him and suddenly felt lighthearted again, and supremely confident in his ability.

When they got back to the car Rafe firmly called it a day and they drove back to Gloucester where Charis sent a note to Mr Carter informing him of the address of the hotel, and where they afterwards had a meal and then went back to the hotel for an early night.

The next morning they set off very early again, before anyone in the hotel was up, and drove to within a mile of the first commune where they left the car and then went on foot, their packs on their backs. They were both dressed in jeans and sweaters with cagoules over the top to keep out the early morning mist. Rafe took a bearing from the map and then set off across country to a point that would bring them out on the hillside overlooking the farm that he had noted the day before. The mist slowly cleared as the sun rose higher in the sky, giving the landscape a slightly blurred, washed-clean look, as if someone had given the earth a good scrub and it hadn't yet dried out. It was very quiet, just the busy sounds of the birds flying round the hedgerows and the swish of their feet brushing through the wet grass. But the smells were intoxicating; the clean fresh fragrance of the grass, the heavy scent of the honeysuckle that clung to the hedgerows like snow in summer, and the sweet perfume of the hundreds of flowers that grew wild beneath the hedges and in the meadows. Despite their errand, Charis experienced a great feeling of contentment, a feeling that she had lived all her life just to be in this place at this moment, that she would like to have it go on for eternity.

She turned to Rafe, silently walking along beside her, and said impulsively, 'Isn't it the most wonderful day!'

His left eyebrow rose quizzically and he gave a rather sardonic smile. 'Yes, I suppose it is.'

Immediately Charis felt crushed, realising that it was a stupid thing to say in the circumstances. Her mood changed completely and she was very close to tears as she turned her face away from Rafe and looked fixedly across the fields.

Neither of them spoke again until they neared the hill overlooking the commune, then Rafe motioned to her to keep low while he took off his pack and went on

alone. He came back in about ten minutes and pointed
further up the hill.

'I think our best position would be up there, among
that clump of trees. We'll be hidden from all sides
there.'

He picked up his pack again and Charis followed
him, taking care to keep below the brow of the hill.
When they got to the trees they found that they formed
a rough circle with a grassy clearing in the centre.

Rafe gave a grunt of satisfaction. 'Couldn't be
better.' He dropped the rucksack and took off his
cagoule, spreading it on the ground where he could
look through a gap in the foliage down to the farm in
the valley.

Charis copied him, settling herself comfortably on
her cagoule with her back against a handy treetrunk.
From here she could see the whole of the farm laid out
before her: the old farmhouse itself with a steeply
pitched, red-tiled roof set here and there with dormer
windows at different levels. Around the farmhouse
there was the usual conglomeration of outhouses, some
built of wood, others of brick and tiles, and around
them all was a high old stone wall with a wooden gate
giving on to a track leading to the lane. There were
roses growing up the walls of the house and in front of
it someone had made a garden, so that, with the sun
shining on it, the whole place had a bland, chocolate-
box lid appearance, as innocent as the picture in a
child's book under 'F' for farm. A far cry from the
megalomaniac doctrine that was now being perpetrated
under its roof in the name of religion.

At first Charis thought that everyone must be still
asleep, but then the lowing of cattle drifted through

the clear air and she saw a man herding half a dozen cows out of the big barn.

'They do their milking early,' Rafe remarked, and she saw that he had his binoculars out and was looking through them. He took a notebook and a pen out of his pocket and, after glancing at his watch, opened it and made a note.

'Why are you doing that?' Charis asked curiously.

'I'm trying to build up a picture of the farm routine by timing everything that happens. After a few days we should be pretty certain of how many people there are and where they'll be at any given time of day.'

As they watched the farm gradually came to life. The man who had been milking the cows came back from taking them out to the fields, sauntering unhurriedly along and whistling as he went. Smoke rose from one of the chimneys and soon after the kitchen door opened and a girl came out and walked over to the chicken run to collect eggs. Charis stiffened when she saw the girl and Rafe quickly handed her the binoculars. For a frustrating few moments she couldn't focus them properly, but then the girl came clearly into view and Charis relaxed and silently shook her head as she handed the glasses back.

More people appeared from time to time; to feed the hens, to hang out washing, a whole group of men climbed on to a tractor and trailer and went off into the fields, a van arrived to deliver groceries and a small lorry came to collect two churns of milk. There seemed to be something happening most of the morning and Rafe was kept busy making notes while Charis' heart stopped every time a girl came into view and only started again when she was sure it wasn't Jane.

Towards the middle of the afternoon things seemed to quieten down and they took the opportunity to finish off the food and drink they had brought with them that they had bought in Gloucester the day before. It was very hot now, the sun beating down on the clearing without even a whiff of breeze to break the stillness.

Rafe stood up. 'I'm going for a walk. Don't forget to write anything you see in the notebook.'

Stretching out on the grass, Charis focused the glasses on the farmhouse and tried to keep alert, but the sun was beating down on her back and she felt hot and heavy-eyed. Her sweater she had discarded long ago and she heartily wished that she had worn shorts and a sun-top instead of jeans and a shirt. Nothing moved on the farm and the only sounds were of crickets in the grass and the buzzing of insects in the still air. Her head nodded, but she jerked awake again. The sound of an engine broke the silence and Charis tensed expectantly, but it was only a car going along the road and it had soon passed and disappeared. She settled back on her elbows and swept the glasses over the farm again in a desultory way, confident that nothing had changed. As she did so, a slight movement near one of the barns caught her eyes and she brought the binoculars back to look more closely. But she must have been mistaken, there was nothing there now. She watched the spot for several minutes and her eyes began to feel heavy again. Then she almost dropped the glasses in shock as she saw Rafe run from behind the barn to the shelter of another building nearer the farmhouse. Hastily, her hands shaking, Charis re-focused the glasses and felt a moment of blind panic when she couldn't see him, but then she lowered them and saw that he had moved to the other corner of the building and was crouching down, partly hidden by the tall undergrowth. What on earth was he doing? Surely he didn't intend to break into the place in broad daylight! As she watched, her fingers tight on the glasses, Rafe turned his head and deliberately looked up in her direction, his eyes scanning the hillside. Was that what he'd gone down there for? she wondered. To find out if they could be seen from the farm?

He seemed satisfied and began to move back the way he had come. Charis gave a great sigh of relief; he was only about twenty yards away from the open back door of the farmhouse and much too close to it for her peace of mind. He shot across the open space between the outbuildings and the barn safely and began to work his way towards some bushes that screened the part of the wall that he had obviously climbed over. Then, just as he neared the end of the barn, a door in its side began to open slowly. Rafe froze, and so did Charis' heart. She watched in fascinated horror as the door was gradually pushed wider, its hinges creaking protestingly. Her mind conjured up all sorts of pictures about who was pushing it, and she didn't know whether to laugh or cry when a small, shaggy-looking dog came through the doorway into the open.

It saw Rafe almost at once, but it was an old dog and had probably just woken up from its afternoon nap, so it wasn't quite with it. It only had time to bark twice before Rafe grabbed it and muzzled it. But it had been enough to make one of the men come to see what was the matter. He stood in the doorway of the farmhouse, whistling and calling the dog, who squirmed and wriggled in Rafe's arms, vainly trying to get free. Charis watched in terror as the man, obviously grumbling to himself, moved out of the doorway and began to cross towards the barn.

Her attention had been so riveted on what was happening in the farmyard that Charis hadn't even heard the noise of an approaching vehicle, but it had turned off the road and up the lane leading to the farm, and now it was at the gate, the driver hooting for someone to come and open it. The man immediately turned and obediently went to answer the summons. The moment he was out of sight, Rafe ran across to the bushes, the dog still held in his arms. Then he released it and within a minute was over the wall. The dog began to bark furiously the moment he was set free, pawing at the wall where Rafe had gone over, but then the animal turned and, still barking, ran over to where the vehicle had driven up in front of the farmhouse.

Someone yelled at the dog to be quiet and Charis' heartbeat returned to normal. Phew! That had been much too close for comfort. There was no sign of Rafe now, he had disappeared behind a hedge, so she gave her attention to the farm again.

The vehicle that had driven in was rather a strange one; it seemed to be half minibus, half van, painted light blue, with windows and seats halfway along at the front but with the rear part boxed in and with ordinary van doors at the back. At the moment it had only the driver in it, but he and the man from the farm went round to the back and began to load it up with what looked like provisions carried from the farmhouse kitchen: trays of eggs and that sort of thing. Picking up the notebook, Charis carefully made a note of its arrival and the time, together with its registration number. It could be that this was the van that the Brotherhood used for transporting supplies from one commune to another—and perhaps the seats meant that it was what they used for transporting people, too.

The van wasn't there long, only about twenty minutes, then the doors were closed and it drove away, back along the road leading to Ciren. A few minutes later Rafe rejoined her in the clearing, coming up so quietly that she didn't hear him until he was quite close and he made her jump. Charis looked at him with mixed feelings; glad that he was safely back but angry that he'd gone down to the farm without telling her.

He took one look at her face and said, 'You saw me, then?'

'It would have been difficult not to. Could you see me—I take it that *was* your reason for going down there?'

'Partly. No, I couldn't see you, but we'll have to be careful as the sun goes round that it doesn't reflect back off the glasses.'

'Why else did you go?'

'To have a scout round. Find out exactly how to use the outbuildings as cover if I wanted to approach the place in the dark. And also,' he added with a hint of satisfaction in his voice, 'to find out if I could still do it.'

Charis looked at him suspiciously. 'That doesn't sound like Operations Management to me!'

He looked at her and grinned, a devilish glint in his blue eyes. 'I wasn't always in charge of operations, I took part in them too.'

'And enjoyed them—as you're enjoying this.'

She hadn't realised that she'd spoken accusingly until she saw the grin fade and his eyes settle on her face. 'I'm not treating it as a game, if that's what you think. I know how you feel about it and, believe me, I'm as serious as you are. But I can't help enjoying a challenge, and that's what this search represents.' He waited a moment, then said questioningly, 'Charis?'

She smiled suddenly. 'You gave me the most terrible fright, especially when the dog barked. Why didn't you tell me you were going down there?'

'You might have tried to stop me,' he returned evenly.

She shook her head. 'No, I wouldn't. You knew the risk you were taking. Besides,' she smiled slightly, 'it wouldn't have done any good, would it?'

He grinned back. 'Not a lot. But it helps to know you trust me.' Their eyes met for a moment, then he turned away and reached for his rucksack. 'Is there any drink left? I'm thirsty.'

'Just a couple of cans of beer, and they're probably warm by now, even though they've been in the shade.'

'Never mind, they'll do.' He pulled back the tab on one and offered it to her. 'Here.'

Charis hesitated, but she, too, was very thirsty. 'I've never drunk beer before.'

'Well, it won't hurt you, and after a while you might even get to like it.'

She took the can and sipped experimentally, pulling a face at first at the bitter taste, but at least it was wet, and she took a good drink before passing it back.

'What did you make of the van?' he asked her after taking a long, thirsty swallow. 'I couldn't see much of it from where I was.'

Charis described it and he agreed with her idea that it could be used for moving converts from one commune to another.

'Sounds reasonable. They probably use this farm as a supply depot for the whole sect. It will be interesting to find out if it comes here every day.' He took another drink and said, 'I found out something myself when I was down there. The back door was open and I managed to see a little way inside. It didn't lead directly into the kitchen but into a little sort of hallway first. And from what I could make out there was a kind of noticeboard fixed to the wall with several papers that looked like lists pinned to it. Which makes me wonder if they were some kind of work rosters with the names of all the people who're at the farm listed on them.'

'And if Jane's isn't there . . .' Charis began following his train of thought.

'Then we'll be able to cross this place off the list and go on to the next.'

'I don't think she is here,' Charis maintained. 'This farm is too open, and we've seen everyone who's here through the glasses. I think they've got her at that other place, Earlswood Hall.'

'Possibly. But I think we ought to make absolutely sure here first.'

'So you're going to go down again and try and take a look at the noticeboard,' Charis said flatly, already knowing the answer. 'How? At night?'

'Perhaps. But I think there might be a better way.'

He wouldn't enlarge on it, saying that he hadn't made up his mind yet, then he yawned and pulled the sports shirt he was wearing over his head. 'Think I'll take a nap. Wake me in an hour, okay? And don't go to sleep.'

Charis looked at him rather indignantly as he stretched out on the grass in the sun, envying him his ability to strip to the waist and wishing she could do the same. She wouldn't have minded a sleep, either, but she obediently picked up the glasses and settled herself more comfortably against the tree trunk. At least the sun had moved round now and she was in the shade. Dutifully she noted down every movement in the farm below, but nothing much was happening, there weren't many animals to see to and it was too early for haymaking.

Her gaze drifted away from the farm and settled on Rafe rather furtively. His chest was broad with a mat of dark hairs growing down to the line of his jeans. He looked lean, almost too lean, but his arms and shoulders were well muscled and she guessed that he had always been very athletic. His skin was pale, but not pallid; as if he'd been tanned a lot in the past but it had faded and not been renewed. She supposed, enviously, that his was the type of skin that just went brown without going through the horrible red stage. Putting a hand up to her own nose, she was sure that the sun had caught it and by tomorrow she would look like Rudolf, the red-nosed reindeer. She continued to study him for a few minutes longer, but then he moved in his sleep and she quickly looked away, a pink flush on her cheeks.

She woke him exactly an hour later, only having to lightly touch him once before his eyes opened and he was immediately alert.

'Anything happened?'

'No, nothing.'

'Okay, your turn to get your head down for a while.'

Charis did so gratefully, using her rolled-up sweater as a pillow, but she didn't stretch out as he had done, instead turning her back on him and curling into a ball, unwilling to expose herself to his gaze when she was vulnerable in sleep, even though she had looked at him. It was different somehow.

Nothing of any interest happened at the farm for the rest of that day. At dusk someone came out and fed the dog which was left to run loose outside, then the lights went on and from the windows, open to let in the coolness of the evening air, they heard the faint sound of singing. Around ten o'clock the lights went out in all but one or two upstairs rooms and Rafe stood up.

'I think we might as well call it a day. There's no point in trying to get into the place tonight without something to keep the dog quiet. We'll come back tomorrow.'

They walked back to the car and drove back to Gloucester, stopping to eat at a café on the way. Charis tumbled straight into bed, grateful that Rafe had said they needn't start out quite so early tomorrow.

But they were again in position behind the screen of bushes by nine the next morning. If anything, the day was even hotter, but this time Charis had come prepared and was wearing a sun-top and shorts under her jeans and sweater, and stripped down to them when the sun got really hot. She caught Rafe running his eyes over her, but he didn't make any comment, merely taking off his own shirt a little later on. Charis saw with envy that she had been right, his skin was already starting to tan.

The routine at the farm was very much as it had been the day before. The grocery van arrived at about the same time, soon followed by the lorry that collected the churns of milk. Rafe looked at the latter thoughtfully and said, 'I wonder if that lorry belongs to the Brotherhood as well or if it's owned by a dairy that collects milk from all the local farms.'

'It's got some writing on the door,' Charis answered as she looked through the binoculars, 'but it's in light brown letters on a dark brown background and it's very faded. I can hardly make it out.' She twisted the focus screw a little more, then, 'Yes, I think you're right, but it's also difficult to see because the van's parked at the wrong angle. I think it says Norton Dairy Co-operative. No, not Norton—Merton, that's it. Merton Dairy Co-operative,' she said triumphantly.

'Good girl. Is there a phone number?'

She shook her head. 'Not that I can see.'

Picking up his shirt, Rafe pulled it over his head and then stood up. 'Take over for a while, will you.'

'Why, where are you going?'

He frowned, as if a subordinate had asked an impertinent question, then grinned wryly at himself and answered, 'I want to go back to that telephone box near where we left the car and make a call.'

'Who to?'

'To the Merton Dairy Co-operative, of course.'

He turned, before she could ask any more questions, and walked briskly away, leaving Charis to wonder what on earth he expected to find out.

It was some while before he came back and the time dragged by. Nothing was happening at the farm and she grew hot and restless, changing her position several

times in an attempt to stay in the shade and still keep
an eye on the farmhouse. When he did return almost
an hour later, she had to contain her impatience until
he had drunk almost half a can of beer in one long,
thirsty swallow. His shirt was stained with perspiration
and he put up a hand to lift the damp locks of hair that
clung to his forehead.

'Phew, I needed that! Who was it said that only mad
dogs and Englishmen go out in the midday sun?'

'Noël Coward,' Charis answered flatly, then, impatiently, 'Well, how did you get on?'

'It wasn't Merton Dairy, it was Homerton Dairy, so
it took some time to find the number. But when I got
through I pretended to be a prospective dairy farmer
and I found out that they send a lorry round to all the
farms every day.'

'So?' Charis asked, still puzzled.

'So,' Rafe answered, the devilish light again in his
eyes, 'the lorry will call here again at the same time
tomorrow morning.' He laughed at her outraged face,
then relented. 'And we, my dearest Charis, are going
to use it as a way into the commune!'

CHAPTER FOUR

RAFE wouldn't tell her any more, but made her collect their things together, leaving out only a couple of cans of drink and the binoculars and notebook.

'What time did that van that we think belongs to the commune arrive yesterday?'

Charis consulted the notebook. 'Almost exactly three o'clock.'

'Good. Here's what we're going to do.' His tone brisk and decisive, Rafe continued, 'I'm going to go back to the car and drive it along the road towards this hill. I want you to keep a look out for it and as soon as it comes in sight move out into the open and wave so that I can see you. Got that?'

Charis looked at him. 'Yes, I've got that,' she replied evenly.

Her tone made him glance up at her face and he grinned. 'Sorry. When I see you I'll pull up and wait. I want to follow the blue van, but unfortunately we don't know which direction it came from yesterday, and there's nowhere near the spot where the farm track leaves the road where we can park the car without being seen, so I'll have to wait round the bend out of sight among the trees. If it comes from the direction of Gloucester, it'll have to pass me, of course, and if it goes back the same way, there's no problem; I'll just fall in behind the van and follow it to find out where it goes next. But if it comes from the other direction and goes back the same way I'll have to rely on you to give me a signal so that I'll know when to follow it.'

'What if it doesn't come today?'

He shrugged philosophically. 'Then we'll think of something else.'

'What do I do if the van comes and you follow it?'

'Give it an hour and then walk back to the place where we parked this morning and wait until I come back for you.'

He left soon after, taking most of their things with him, and Charis gave him twenty minutes before moving to the other side of the clearing, away from the farmhouse, where she could see the road. It was more of a lane really, bounded by hedgerows broken here and there by clumps of trees and the occasional farm gate. Below the hill it curved in a wide bend that covered about a quarter of a mile, and from where she stood she could see the whole length laid out before her, starting from the Gloucester end where the trees were quite thick and going on to where the farm track met the road and the land was much more open with only quite low hedges, and then on again in the direction of the old Roman town of Cirencester.

She waited, sweater ready in her hand, and hoped she wouldn't wave at the wrong car. A small green van went noisily along the road in a tearing hurry and then a man pedalling slowly by on a bicycle, reminding Charis of the hare and the tortoise. Then a blue car came into sight, dawdling along, and she moved out of the shelter of the trees and waved like mad. The car flashed its lights at her and pulled off the road under the cover of the trees. Charis went back across the clearing and waited to see if the commune's van would come.

It did, but it was later today, it was almost four before it came trundling up the track and hooted imperiously at the gate. Charis watched while it loaded up and turned to go back, then ran through the clearing to her vantage point on the other side of the hill. The van turned to the left out of the track and headed towards Cirencester. Charis waved her sweater again and saw Rafe pull out from the trees and follow it.

When Rafe came back for her over two hours later, she was sitting patiently on the grass at the side of the road. He pushed open the passenger door for her and she climbed in beside him with a sigh of relief.

'Fed up with waiting?' Rafe asked quizzically.

'No,' Charis replied rather tersely. 'I was just getting tired of refusing lifts into Gloucester.'

His eyebrows rose. 'Were you, by God?'

'The natives round here seem to be extremely friendly,' Charis explained.

His eyes ran over her again, taking in her long, bare legs and slim, but very feminine figure. 'I don't blame them.'

Charis felt herself starting to blush and asked hastily, 'Did you manage to follow the van?'

His blue eyes amused, Rafe said, 'Yes. As I'd hoped, it went straight from the farm to the other commune we looked at, Earlswood Hall. I waited about for a while, but it didn't come out again, so presumably it's kept there permanently.'

'I don't see how that's going to help us,' Charis objected.

'It may not. But the more information we have about the communes the easier it will be to decide what to do.'

'So what are we going to do?' Charis demanded.

He looked at her speculatively for a moment, then

said, 'Tomorrow we're going to go to the bank and draw out some money, and then I'm going to try and bribe the driver of the milk churn lorry to let me take it into the farmyard. Then I'll make sure that I get into that hallway and get a look at the list of names.'

Charis stared at him open-mouthed, overwhelmed by the simplicity of the idea. But then all sorts of problems came to mind. 'But what if he won't be bribed? And what if they won't let you into the house? Suppose they catch you reading the lists? Do you *know* how to drive a lorry?' she finished on an accusing note.

He laughed. 'Yes, of course I can drive a lorry. And as for the lorry driver—if he won't be bribed, then I'll try to play on his sympathy.'

'How?'

'By telling him the truth, near enough. Only I'll say that it's my girl-friend I'm trying to find. And I'll get into the house by quite simply asking to use the loo. They can hardly refuse that request, now can they?'

'What if they want to know where the regular driver is?'

'I'll tell them that he's off sick today,' Rafe answered promptly.

Charis looked at him with awe. 'You know, Rafe, you really have a devious mind. I'd never have thought of all those lies.'

'Oh, please, it's nothing,' he replied with mock modesty. 'They give you a very comprehensive training in the Army.' Then he looked at her sideways and they both burst out laughing.

But Charis was far from laughter the next morning as they waited for the lorry from the dairy to come along. Rafe had parked the car in the same layby on the Gloucester road that they had used on the last two days, knowing that the lorry had to pass that way before going to the farm. Neither of them spoke very much; Rafe was leaning nonchalantly against the side of the car, apparently quite unperturbed, but Charis couldn't keep still; she kept moving nervously away, glancing back along the road every time she heard a car, or thought she heard one.

Rafe watched her for a while, then said, 'Relax. There's nothing for you to worry about.'

'No, of course not.' She came over to lean against the car next to him, but was only there for a few minutes before straightening up and starting to move away again.

But Rafe caught her arm and stopped her. 'Stop worrying! If this doesn't work we'll try something else.'

'I'm not worried about it not working,' Charis told him, her eyes widening in surprise. 'I'm worried that they might catch you reading the notices at the farm and—and hurt you.'

Rafe looked at her intently for a moment, then said brusquely, 'No one's going to hurt me.'

'How do you know? We counted at least six men living at the farm.'

His tone sardonic, Rafe answered, 'The sect are believers in peace, not violence, remember? And anyway, I can take care of myself.'

'Oh, but . . .'

He rounded on her suddenly, his voice rough. 'Taking risks is what you're paying me for, isn't it?'

Charis' face paled and she looked hastily down at the ground, her hands balled into tight fists at her sides.

After a moment, Rafe muttered, 'Oh, hell! Look, I

didn't mean to upset you. I . . .'

'Oh, I'm not upset. Of course I'm not. You're quite right, I'm afraid I always tend to worry about—about people I'm with.' She said it firmly enough, but her eyes were over-bright when she at last lifted them to look at him.

'Then maybe it's about time you let someone else do the worrying for a change,' Rafe told her harshly.

Charis looked at him in surprise; the idea that someone might worry about her had never occurred to her before. She was about to speak when the sound of an engine reached them and they both tensed. The milk churn lorry came into sight and Rafe said quickly, 'Go and wait in the car. If I need you I'll call you.'

She obeyed without question and watched as Rafe moved out into the middle of the road and put his hand up to stop the lorry. It pulled up at the side of the road and he went round to talk to the driver. He was there for some time, then the driver got out and they talked some more, or rather Rafe did the talking while the driver listened. Then some money changed hands and Rafe climbed up into the cab of the lorry and drove away while the driver came over to the car.

'Your friend said I could wait here with you.'

'Yes, of course.'

'I knew as how they were a lot of religious freaks in that place,' he told her as he sat beside her. He was approaching middle age, a rather fat man with crinkly dark hair. 'It shouldn't be allowed. They ought to pass a law or something to stop young kids joining that kind of thing. He said she was your sister?'

'Yes, that's right. She's only nineteen.'

'Shouldn't be allowed,' he repeated. 'I've got a couple of kids of me own.'

Charis encouraged him to talk, grateful for his sympathy and that he hadn't asked too many questions. She made comments every now and again, but she wasn't really listening at all, her mind was too busy imagining just what Rafe was doing at that moment and, not being much of an optimist, fearing the worst.

Twenty agonisingly long minutes later, the lorry appeared round the bend and Charis shot out of the car. Rafe pulled up and jumped out of the cab and she grabbed his arm before he even reached the ground.

'Are you all right? Did they catch you? Was her name on the list?'

He shook his head. 'No. No luck, I'm afraid. They had several rosters for different jobs on the board, but Jane's name wasn't on any of them. I think we can cross the farm off the list and go on to the next place.'

The driver came over and commiserated with them. He talked for a few minutes longer, then shook hands and went on his way.

'Did they suspect you?' Charis asked when they were alone.

He shook his head. 'Not a bit. The downstairs cloakroom was just off that hallway and I had plenty of time to look at the board.'

'So what do we do now? Try Earlswood Hall? That won't be so easy to get into.'

'Maybe it will,' Rafe told her. 'I've got an idea that just might work.'

The next day was Sunday and Rafe suggested that they take a walk round the town centre, saying that there wasn't a lot they could do that day as all the shops were, of course, closed, and he needed to buy some equipment before they went any further. The morning was beautiful, a perfect English early summer day, with just a slight breeze to temper the heat of the sun. Charis put on a brightly coloured summer dress and high-heeled sandals, perfectly happy to take a day off after the tension of yesterday. The town was quite busy, everyone seemed to want to be out of doors on such a lovely day, and there were quite a few tourists to add to the throng. Most people were heading in the general direction of the huge cathedral and Charis and Rafe turned to follow them at a leisurely pace, more for somewhere to go than anything else.

The great doors of the cathedral were wide open and Charis blinked as she walked from the bright sunlight into the dim interior. It was very old and very high, the supporting pillars soaring ever upwards in great columns of stone to where the beautifully carved roof looked like delicate lacework, so intricately had it been fashioned. There was a hushed murmur of noise everywhere as the visitors lowered their voices in automatic reverence for the antiquity and sacredness of the building, but every now and again a child would speak in a high, piping voice which would echo round the aisles, and right up into the highest point of the roof. They moved on and then both came to a tacit stop as they gazed up at the stained-glass window set into the east wall of the cathedral. It was huge, seventy-two feet high by almost forty wide, and was a riot of brilliant colours pieced into dozens of pictures, all of which were reflected on the stone floor as the sun shone through the great window.

'It's the largest medieval stained glass window in

England,' Rafe told her, pointing towards a brass tablet on the wall.

Charis nodded, unable to speak. She stood there for a long time, then closed her eyes as if the colour was too much to take. Please, oh, please let me find Jane and bring her home, she prayed—a prayer she had made many times before, but somehow it seemed more cogent in these surroundings. She felt Rafe touch her arm and opened her eyes to find him looking at her intently, a frown between his brows.

'Let's get out of here,' he said abruptly, and quickly led her out into the sunshine again.

They found a pub by the river that did snack lunches and sat at a wooden picnic table to watch all the activity on the river: pleasure boats, fishermen, canoeists, swimmers—there was almost as much going on in the river as there was in the town. Afterwards they strolled along beside the water under the dappled shade of the trees.

'I'll get the stuff I need in the morning,' Rafe remarked, 'and by tomorrow night, with any luck, we'll know if Jane's at Earlswood Hall.'

'So soon?' Charis looked at him in surprise. 'But how will you get in there?'

'I'm going to get a lift from the Brotherhood's own van.' And he grinned at her look of bafflement, then, seeing the gleam of indignation that came into her grey eyes, he began to explain.

When he had finished Charis stopped and turned to look at him in awe. 'I'd *never* have thought of that! I was right, you do have a devious mind.'

'Nonsense. That's what's known as lateral thinking; indispensable if you want to get on in this day and age.'

Charis laughed at him and turned to go on, but then

her face changed completely and she grabbed Rafe's arm. 'Look! Behind you,' she said urgently. 'Those two young men coming towards us—I've seen them before. They were at the Brotherhood's headquarters in Bristol when I went down to try and find Jane. I tried to get them to tell me where she was, but they wouldn't.'

Rafe glanced swiftly round, saw that the two youths were almost up to them and, before Charis knew what was happening, pushed her back against a tree and kissed her.

She made an involuntary movement to push him away, but his arms came round her, pinning her arms to her sides, forcing her to be still, his body leaning against her so that she couldn't move. She opened her mouth to utter a squawk of protest, but as her lips opened she felt his mouth pressing against hers with restrained softness and the protest died in her throat. Her eyes closed and slowly the rigidity left her body and she became aware of his strength, imprisoning her, moulding her body to his.

When he lifted his head she slowly opened her eyes and looked into his blue ones, so close to her own. His expression was completely enigmatic, unreadable.

Still holding her, he said, 'Charis is a very unusual name. I've not heard it before.'

'It's Greek,' she told him, her voice unsteady. 'It's another name for any one of the three Graces.'

'Is it?' he answered casually, and bent to kiss her again.

This time she didn't look at him, but lowered her head and said huskily, 'Why did you do that?'

Rafe straightened up and let her go. 'Those two men—if you recognised them, there was a good chance that they might also recognise you, so I thought I'd better hide your face.'

'Oh! Yes, of course.' Charis glanced after the youths and saw that they were about fifty yards or so away. 'Are we going to follow them?'

'If you like, but I don't think we'll learn much from them: they're probably out looking for likely converts.'

They began to walk in the same direction as the young men, going back towards the town centre, and presently they saw them go into a snack bar where jukebox music could be heard coming through the open door. For a quarter of an hour or so they hung around outside, but then Rafe said he didn't think they'd learn much even if they did follow the two members of the Brotherhood.

'But we didn't see them at the farm,' Charis reminded him, 'so they've probably come from Earlswood Hall. They'll know if Jane is there.'

'Yes, but they wouldn't tell you before, so they're not likely to now. And if you spoke to them they might get alarmed and move Jane, or lock her up somewhere, which would spoil all our plans for tomorrow,' Rafe reminded her gently, taking her arm and drawing her away.

Charis hung back, looking at the snack bar helplessly, then fell in beside him. 'You're right, of course. I'm sorry.'

'It's understandable. I'd feel the same way if it was someone I loved who was shut away. I'd want to get hold of them and wring their necks until they told me where she was.'

'That's *exactly* how I feel,' Charis said forcefully. 'I could have *hit* them when they wouldn't tell me!'

Rafe's eyebrows came up at that and he laughed. 'What a bloodthirsty little thing you are, and here was I thinking you were the timid type!'

'Well, I suppose I am, really,' she admitted. 'But I'll fight if I have to.'

His eyes rested on her thoughtfully. 'I really believe you would.'

They wandered round Gloucester's tourist attractions for an hour or so longer, then had a meal and went to the cinema, returning to their hotel about eleven. Charis went straight to bed but couldn't sleep, even though she was tired from their day in the sun. Inevitably she worried about tomorrow, but tried to put it out of her mind, encouraged by the success Rafe had had yesterday in getting into the farm. She was well pleased with the way things were going so far, never having expected to cross even one commune off their list this early, even though she hadn't really expected Jane to be there. She knew she wouldn't have stood a chance of being so successful herself and could only be thankful that she'd found someone as resourceful as Rafe to help her. By now she had complete faith in his ability to find Jane and to get her out if it was at all possible. If it was possible. Her mind edged away from pessimism and somehow found its way back to that afternoon when Rafe had kissed her. Only another example of his resourcefulness, of course. Nothing more. But it made her wonder what it would be like if he had kissed her because he really wanted to. And she couldn't help wondering, also, just why he had found it necessary to kiss her twice. And she was still thinking about it when she fell asleep half an hour later.

CHAPTER FIVE

At nine the next morning, Rafe went to one of the many boat chandlers along the river and bought a length of rope, then on to a hardware shop to buy some stout gloves and a pair of wire cutters. In the meanwhile Charis had gone into other shops to get their usual supply of food and drink to put in their backpacks. They met up again back at the hotel, where Charis found a letter waiting for her from Mr Carter. In it he enclosed her provisional driving licence, saying that he had personally gone to the appropriate office to collect it for her as she had said that she wanted it urgently. For a moment Charis had a mental picture of the well-ordered London office where Mr Carter presided over his staff, dealing with his clients' problems in a calm, efficient manner. She liked and respected him, but he wasn't the kind of man she could get close to, who could in any way take the place of a parent.

'Good,' Rafe said approvingly when she showed him the licence. 'We'll stop at the nearest garage for some L-plates and I'll give you your first lesson this morning.'

He kept his threat, too, making her get into the driving seat at the garage and take over the car. Charis thanked her lucky stars that the road was a quiet and completely empty minor one, because she had a feeling that he would have made her do the same even if it was in the middle of a town. For a while they moved up the road in jerks and stops, as if they'd got 'kangaroo' petrol, Rafe informed her dryly, but she soon got the hang of the gears and she managed to drive the car without stalling it more than once a mile. But then, just as she was starting to feel quite confident, he made her practise stopping and starting off, which wasn't anywhere near so easy as just steering. He kept her at it for about an hour, then took over the wheel himself. Charis was glad; she sat back in the passenger seat feeling hot and on edge, her lips dry and her head aching from concentrating so hard.

Rafe looked at her and smiled, not unsympathetically. 'You did well,' he assured her. 'Don't worry, it'll be easier the next time.'

'Oh, I hope so,' she answered fervently. 'I'm so hot. Do you think we could stop and have a drink?'

Glancing at his watch, he answered. 'Okay. We might as well have our lunch now, anyway.'

He pulled off the road into the entrance to a field and they got out their picnic. While they ate Rafe made her repeat exactly what she had to do that night until he was satisfied she had it right. When she had finished he nodded approvingly. 'Good girl, it should go like clockwork.' He grinned at her and, caught by the devilish look of enjoyment in his eyes, she grinned back, all doubts and worries for the moment lost. He glanced at his watch again. 'Okay, let's go.'

They drove out as near as they could get to Earlswood Hall and parked the car out of sight, then walked along under the cover of the high wall with its barbed-wire top, looking for a tree that overhung it, but found that all the branches had been neatly lopped back, so they had to make do with a tall oak tree which grew only a few yards away from the wall.

'This should do. Keep watch while I shin up and have a look.'

Rafe climbed the tree with surprising ease, the binoculars round his neck. He stayed up there for a few minutes, then came down again and tied the rope securely round the trunk of the tree, testing the knot by putting his weight on it, and afterwards carefully coiling the rest of the rope and hiding it behind a leafy bush.

He stood back and surveyed his handiwork. 'That should be okay,' he muttered. 'No one walking by can see the rope.'

He set a good pace on the way back and Charis had to hurry to keep up with him; his leg didn't seem to trouble him at all. When they reached the car, Rafe took off the L-plates and drove to a road which they knew the Brotherhood's van would have to pass along on its daily journey from the farm to Earlswood Hall. He pulled into the side and released the bonnet clip, got out and did something to the engine, then pulled on a black sweater over his shirt.

'You know what you've got to do?' Charis nodded and he looked her over appraisingly. 'Don't forget to smile at him—and let him see your legs,' he added, his eyes running over them, all the way up to the start of her white shorts.

'Why?' she demanded indignantly.

Rafe's left eyebrow rose cynically. 'Be your age, woman! The driver might not stop for a broken-down car, but he'll certainly stop and offer to help if he sees a pretty girl with a lovely pair of legs.'

'Oh.'

Charis started to colour up, but Rafe went on briskly, 'I'll walk down to the bend now and signal you when he's coming. If he's on schedule he should be along in about twenty minutes. Whatever you do,' he added warningly, 'don't let any other motorist stop and help you. That would ruin everything.'

He walked down the tree-lined road to the bend and Charis sat in the driving seat of the car to wait. It was still intensely hot, but there was a stillness in the atmosphere today that presaged a big storm that would end the heatwave. Her hands were hot and sticky as they gripped the steering-wheel nervously, her eyes glued to Rafe's figure as he stood, partly hidden by a large tree, on the other side of the road. A car came into view and she looked away, praying it wouldn't stop, but it passed safely by. Then there was a long gap before a farm tractor trundled noisily along the road, travelling agonisingly slowly. Charis waited for it to pass in trepidation; what if the van came along while it was still in sight? It would look most peculiar to the tractor driver if she went into her act while he was watching.

But eventually he disappeared down the road and she was just heaving a sigh of relief when she saw Rafe wave his arms at her. Hastily she got out of the car and lifted up the bonnet, then leaned over the engine and pretended to be peering into it. She heard the sound of the van's engine and knew that by now Rafe was running back through the trees to where he hoped it would stop. If it stopped. Charis felt herself growing rigid with tension as the noise grew louder. He hadn't even slowed down. He was going to go right past! She stood up and turned to face the approaching van, sticking her chest out and looking towards it with what she hoped was a 'lady in distress' expression.

The van's brakes squeaked noisily but very satisfactorily as it pulled up a few yards further down on the other side.

The driver was quite young, probably in his late twenties, and was wearing a ragged pair of denim shorts and a green tee-shirt with 'Love and Peace' in big white letters on it. He had a moustache and his hair was quite long, tied back with a beaded band round his forehead, like a Red Indian. He strolled across to her and said, 'Having trouble?'

Charis looked at him with a mixture of gratitude and helplessness. 'It won't start.'

'Let's have a go.' He got into the driving seat and turned the ignition key, obviously thinking her incapable of even being able to start it properly. Charis moved to stand beside him, completely blocking his view across the road.

Behind her she heard a slight noise as the door of the van was opened and she began to say loudly, 'I was just driving along and it stopped. It seems to be completely dead. The engine isn't firing at all.'

After one or two experimental turns he admitted that she was right and got out to look under the bonnet. Charis shot a quick glance across the road and just saw Rafe's head ducking down behind one of the empty seats. So he'd hidden in the front of the van and not in the enclosed part at the back. For a bewildered moment she couldn't think why he'd chosen the more open part, until she realised that the first thing the driver would do when he got to the Hall was to open the back doors to take out the provisions.

'Ah, there's your trouble.'

She hurriedly gave the driver her attention. 'You've found what's wrong? Oh, how marvellous!'

'It was simple,' he told her, enjoying her praise. 'The connector on your battery had come loose. It only needs putting back again.' He did so, shut the bonnet and wiped his greasy fingers on his shorts. 'It'll be okay now, but you'd better try it to make sure.'

Charis got in and turned the key, the engine started at once. 'Oh, thank you so much. You are clever. It was so kind of you to stop.' He came to lean in the window and she turned the engine off.

'Live round here, do you?' he asked, his eyes on her bare legs.

'Oh, no. I'm just visiting the area.'

'Really?' His eyes grew more interested. 'Maybe we could meet some time, then. We could go out for a meal and you could tell me all about yourself.'

'But I don't . . .'

'Here by yourself, are you?' he added with studied casualness.

Charis realised suddenly in what direction he was heading and said firmly, 'No, I'm with my mother and father, my two brothers *and* my boy-friend,' she threw in for good measure, seeing with satisfaction the disappointed look that came into his eyes. 'Well, I mustn't keep you. Thanks again for coming to my rescue.'

'That's okay.' He straightened up. 'Off you go, then.'

For a moment blind panic filled her as she realised that he was going to wait and watch her drive away. And she'd only had her first lesson that morning! Now what was she going to do? She'd be bound to stall or crash into a tree and he'd know straightaway that she was a learner. A mental scream for help filled her brain and her thoughts flew to Rafe, hiding in the van. It came to her suddenly that if he had heard, he would probably just expect her to get on with it. Grimly she gritted her teeth and started the engine again, then carefully found first gear and remembered to release the handbrake before she started off. She moved slowly off down the road, keeping as straight as she could and praying that the darn thing wouldn't stall before she got round the bend. Her hands gripped the wheel fiercely and it took all her courage, when the engine began to scream protestingly, to take her hand off the wheel and change gear. She did it much too slowly, but fortunately the engine kept on going and then she was round the corner out of sight and could pull into the side, the car jerking to a stop and the engine stalling as she forgot to take it out of gear.

For a few seconds she had to just sit and wait for her hands to stop trembling, but then the thought of Rafe, hiding in the van, made her jump out of the car and somehow propel her unsteady legs back to the bend she had just come round, where she hid behind a bush to look back up the road. It was all right, the van had gone, Rafe hadn't been discovered. Charis gave a sigh of relief and walked slowly back to the car, feeling almost listless after the release of so much tension. Now she had a long and boring wait ahead of her until it was time to meet Rafe again.

She hesitated by the car, wondering whether to while away some of the time sitting in it and listening to the radio, but the day was so close that she needed to be in the open air. They had only brought one backpack today and, for the third time, Charis carefully checked that she had everything: the gloves and wirecutters, pencil torch, map, sweater, jeans, cagoule, food and drink, pen and paper, although why Rafe had insisted on bringing the latter she didn't know. Luckily the road had a wide, flat verge which she had managed to drive on to, so Charis was able to lock up the car and leave it, confident that it wouldn't be an obstruction to other motorists. If anyone noticed it they would probably think that the owners had left it to go for a walk in the countryside. Which was just what she was going to do. Shouldering the pack, Charis set off on a circular route that would eventually bring her to Earlswood Hall.

It was a long way, about five miles by this indirect route, but she didn't hurry, there was plenty of time. Her thoughts, of course, were mainly on Rafe, wondering whether he'd been found when the van got to the Hall, or whether he'd managed to creep out and hide somewhere. Somehow she didn't have much confidence in the Brotherhood's professed love of peace if they found a prowler in their commune, and she was afraid they would gang up on Rafe and hurt him. That it would take several men to do it she accepted without conscious thought, so sure was she of Rafe's ability to defend himself, but even so she couldn't help worrying.

There were very few people about; a few vehicles passed her as she walked along the road, but after she climbed over a stile on to a public footpath she saw only one or two other walkers and some farmhands in a field who were working desperately hard to cut the harvest of ripe corn, their eyes often going up to the sky, which had become very hazy even though the sun was still shining and it was very hot. Charis watched them as she stopped for a few minutes to rest. Her hair clung damply to her forehead and she could feel prickles of perspiration down her back. Phew! It would be a relief when the storm finally broke, although it would be better from their point of view if it at least held off until tomorrow. She, too, looked anxiously up at the sky; it wouldn't be very pleasant if they had to walk back through the rain tonight.

Pulling out the map, she checked on the rest of the route and then walked unhurriedly on. The path led across the ridge of a hill and she had a superb view of the countryside stretching like a patchwork quilt of green and gold fields across the valley and up to the purple hills on the other side. A small river ran along the bottom of the valley and here the trees were thicker, with the occasional cluster of houses wherever a bridge crossed the flowing waters. Crickets chirped in the long grass beside the path and butterflies vied with the bees to settle on the yellow-eyed daisies and purple clover. The scenery was so beautiful that often her feet slowed and she just stood and gazed, drinking in every detail and fervently wishing that she could live in the country, be able to see views like this every day. But then reality would force its way back into her reluctant mind and she would sigh and walk on, until the scent of a wild rose bush filled her nostrils and she stopped again to carefully pick a blossom so that she could carry the perfume along with her.

After a couple of miles she turned off the right of way where there used to be a gate into a field, but the gate had disappeared, the posts which had held it lying on the ground. The field had already been harvested and the stubble pricked her bare ankles, so she made a detour round the edge and picked up the track again at the other side. Over to her right she saw a cloud of smoke rising into the still air and thought at first that there was a fire, but then she noticed figures moving at the edge of the flames and realised that the farmer must be burning off the stubble in another field—a practice that met with a lot of opposition from conservationists who protested strongly that it harmed the wildlife, both flora and fauna.

As she climbed the fence to get out of the field, Charis glanced down into the next valley and grew suddenly still. About half a mile away, looking timeless and peaceful, were the roofs and gables of Earlswood Hall. Sunlight reflected on the latticed windows like crystal and she stood for several minutes, wondering behind which one of them her sister was living and in what sort of physical and mental state she was in. Her eyes turned to where a small lake lay shimmering in the sun and then on to the trees beyond it. Was Rafe hiding among their shelter, she wondered, waiting for darkness to fall so that he could get close enough to see into the house?

She found the tree they had tied the rope to without difficulty, and rather wearily took off the backpack and sat down to rest. Only six o'clock. Still about four hours to wait before it got really dark now that the days were so long. She ate a couple of sandwiches and finished off the bottle of Coke, then settled down to wait as patiently as she could, but her eyes kept going to the wall, wondering what was going on behind it and wishing that she could see over. If only she could find something to stand on she might be able to see. After a while she got up and began to search around in the undergrowth for a log or branch of wood that she could use. But the search proved fruitless and she stood in frustration until she remembered the fallen gateposts she had passed on the way. But that was over half a mile back and the posts had looked heavy. Almost she rejected the idea, but then she shrugged—after all, what else had she got to do?

The log *was* heavy. After dragging it for only a hundred yards Charis had to stop and take a long rest. The air seemed even closer now that evening had come. Her tee-shirt clung to her damply and beads of per-spiration ran down her face. She wiped them off and picked up one end of the log again; now that she had started she had no intention of giving up. It was quicker to go across the field, even though the stubble scratched her ankles, but once through the fence the other side the going was easier because the way ran downhill and she could drop the log and roll it with her feet. It was well past seven o'clock when she got back to the wall and propped the log on end against it, wedged in place with some stones. It was about four feet high, just right for her to be able to climb up on and look over. She did so very gingerly, crouching down and just peeping over the top in case there was anyone about. She could see right up to the house, but the grounds seemed to be deserted, she couldn't see a soul. Perhaps they were all inside having their evening meal? She stayed up there for a little while trying to spot Rafe among the trees, then gave up and climbed down, contenting herself with breaking the monotony of the long wait by just taking a look every half-hour or so until at last darkness came.

It seemed to come so slowly, and her eyes were so attuned to the gathering dusk, that for some time Charis wasn't sure that it was completely dark, but then she saw lights on in the Hall and realised that the shapes of the trees had become lost in the night. Taking the gloves and wirecutters from the knapsack, she climbed up on her perch again. The idea had been that when Rafe signalled her she would throw the rope over the wall and he would climb up it, take the gloves and cutters that she would hand up to him, and then cut the wire so that he could get over the wall. But now that Charis was up here she could reach the wire quite easily and decided to do the job herself. Putting on the gloves, she carefully cut through the four strands of wire close to the supporting upright, then bent them back a couple of feet along, out of the way. She put the things back in the pack, uncoiled the rope and climbed up with it, ready to let it down on the other side of the wall when Rafe signalled.

The night was as hot and oppressive as the day had been. She had put on her jeans, but it was much too hot for a sweater. Over in the Hall, Charis could see that all the windows were open to let in what little cool air there was. No moon shone and the sky seemed very dark; there was a sort of electricity in the atmosphere that might break out into lightning at the smallest spark. She waited for an hour before the signal came, watching the house and sometimes noticing figures pass in front of the windows, seeing some lights go off and others go on. It was a large house; the sect must have plenty of money to afford its upkeep and that of the other communes, although the farm was probably self-sufficient. A niggling worry that the house might be so big that Rafe wouldn't be able to see all its occupants entered her mind, but she tried to dismiss it; he had been quite confident that if Jane was there he would see her.

When she first heard the owl hoot somewhere in the trees it didn't penetrate, but then it sounded again a couple of minutes later, nearer this time and with a more compelling note to it. Oh! Hastily she let down the rope, her heart racing. She hardly saw Rafe until he was almost up to the wall. He had on one of those black skiing hoods that pulled down over the face leaving holes for the eyes and mouth, and that, together with his black sweater and jeans, made him look extremely sinister.

He shinned up the rope, his head jerking up in surprise when he saw her looking over the wall. 'How on earth did you get up there? You gave me the hell of a start!'

'Well, I wouldn't fancy running into you on a dark night in that hood thing either!'

He bent for a minute, came up with the end of the rope which he looped round the barbed wire upright so that he was standing in a kind of loop, then pulled off the hood and looked at her, one eyebrow raised. 'Well? Don't you want to know if I found her?'

'I'm afraid to ask.'

He grinned suddenly and put his hand over hers. 'She's there! I saw her quite clearly. There's no mistake; she's more like you than you think.'

'Oh, Rafe!' For a moment she could only stare at him, then she said, 'Oh, Rafe!' again and impulsively leaned forward and kissed him. Realisation of what she was doing came a moment later and she began to draw back, but found that he had put a hand behind her head and was holding it firmly in place.

When he let her go a couple of minutes later she was breathless, but he laughed and said, 'I feel like Pyramus and Thisbe!'

'How did she look? Was she all right? Where did you see her?'

'You always ask at least three questions at a time,' he complained. 'And this is hardly the place to have a discussion; it's rather a strain on the arms. Just how *did* you get up there?' he added, trying to peer over the wall.

'I climbed up on a log.'

'Well, jump down again, find the paper and pen and write a note to Jane telling her that you're here and asking her to come with me to talk to you.'

Charis stared at him open-mouthed. 'You mean . . . You mean . . .'

'I mean exactly what I said. If you don't close your mouth,' he added conversationally, 'I shall have to kiss it again.'

She shut it hastily, took another dazed look at his face, then jumped down and scrabbled in the bag for the torch, pen and paper. The note was hurried but as persuasive as she could make it, begging her sister to trust Rafe and come out to talk to her. 'Please come,' she finished, 'just to let me know for certain that you're well and happy, that you're staying here of your own free will.'

She finished the letter and climbed up the log again to give it to him. 'What if she won't come with you?'

'Then I think we'll have to make her.' He pulled the hood on, turning him into a sinister stranger again.

'Do you know where she is?'

'Yes, her room's on . . .'

His words were drowned by a sudden violent clap of thunder. There was no lightning to presage it and Charis almost fell off her log with fright, but Rafe grabbed her arm and she regained her balance. The lightning came then, tearing the sky apart and lighting up the grounds of the Hall as if it was midday instead of midnight, leaving them feeling naked and exposed.

'Keep down,' Rafe ordered tersely. 'I'll be back as soon as I can.'

'But the storm?'

'It might help. Leave the rope.'

And then he was gone, letting out the rope and running to the trees before the next flash of lightning came. Another great clap of thunder rolled across the sky, hardly dying away before the next began. The lightning, too, seemed almost continuous, forking across the sky in jagged streaks of electricity that reached down almost to the roof of the Hall. From somewhere a dog began to howl with fright and a door banged. Forgetting his order to stay down, Charis saw Rafe's dark figure silhouetted for a moment as he ran across the open lawn towards the house. At the same moment she saw a square of light as a door opened in one of the wings of the building and a man looked out. From that angle it was impossible for Rafe to have seen him, and impossible for the man not to have seen Rafe. Charis saw the man stiffen, rush back into the house and come out again a minute later with what looked like a heavy bar in his hand, and then start to run after Rafe, the thunder covering the noise of his pursuit.

Without knowing quite how she had got there, Charis found herself dropping to the ground on the other side of the wall. The lightning was her friend now as she raced desperately through the trees. For a few precious seconds she got entangled with a prickly bush, but then she had pushed her way through it and was running on, faster than she'd ever run in her life. Another flash of lightning showed her that Rafe had reached the house and was just starting to climb the ivy that grew thickly up the wall. The man had stopped at the corner and was peering round it to see where Rafe was. As soon as he saw him he began to run silently across the grass towards him, raising the weapon he carried as he did so. Desperately Charis dashed after him and jumped on his back just as he was about to bring the metal bar down on Rafe's unprotected head. But the shock of having her land on his back threw him off balance and the blow caught Rafe on the shoulder. He didn't cry out, but it must have hurt him, because he lost his grip on the ivy and fell heavily to the ground.

The man let out a bellow of surprise and Charis hastily put one arm across his mouth, afraid that he would call for help, the other she put across his eyes, wrapping her legs round his waist and hanging grimly on as he twisted and spun, trying to grab hold of her and pull her off, but impeded by his iron bar. He caught hold of the arm over his eyes and started to twist her wrist, so she bit him hard on the ear until he let go. It couldn't last, of course. He was a big and powerful man and soon gave a sudden violent jerk that dislodged her legs from round his waist, and then she found herself thrown violently on the grass. Gamely she got up and started forward again, but then a voice said, 'It's all right, darling. Leave him to me,' and Rafe moved past her to hit the man an almighy blow on the chin as he opened his mouth to yell for help.

The fight was quite short; they grappled with each other as the thunder reverberated around them, but the poor man didn't really stand a chance against Rafe's unarmed combat training and was soon lying stunned on the grass. But even as Rafe straightened up from looking at him they heard another man shout from the open doorway. 'Tony? Tony, where are you?'

Rafe swore, then ran over to her and caught her arm. 'Are you all right?' She nodded and he said, 'Good girl! Come on, we've got to get out of here fast.'

They began to run back through the trees, but once again the lightning proved their enemy and lit up their running figures. The man in the house gave a yell and Charis glanced back over her shoulder to see several people running out of the doorway. Already winded, Charis was soon out of breath, but Rafe helped her along and almost lifted her bodily over the wall when at last they reached it. She went over anyhow, catching her foot on one of the loose ends of barbed wire as she did so, and almost falling down the other side. Rafe was immediately behind her, his breath coming in sharply as the wire caught him. Then he was beside her and pulling the rope after him.

'Get the knapsack,' he commanded tersely. 'Make sure you've got everything.'

Another jagged flash of lightning enabled Charis to obey him, while Rafe bent the barbed wire back into

place, threw the log into the undergrowth, and untied
and rolled up the rope.

'Okay?'

'Yes.'

He took the knapsack from her and slung it over his
shoulder together with the coil of rope, then headed
through the trees in the direction that she'd come that
morning.

'Aren't we going back along the road?' Charis
ventured. 'It would be much quicker.'

'No, they'll expect us to go that way and might come
after us in a car. We'll take the longer but safer route.'

Only now, as she hurried along in his wake, did
Charis become fully aware of the ferocity of the storm.
From the first clap of thunder she had been too busy
with her own affairs to realise just how savagely the
sky was being rent apart by the streaks of lightning,
just how loudly the thunder was exploding through
the night. But now she saw it in all its primitive violence and was afraid. She ran after Rafe's hurrying
figure, glad to be out of the trees and in the open, but
at the same time feeling more exposed to the elements.
Glancing back over her shoulder as they reached the
ridge of the hill, Charis saw that there were lights on
all over the Hall now and she could see the headlights
of a car flickering through the trees in the lane leading
past the entrance. Had they found the place where
they'd got over the wall yet? she wondered. Were some
of the Brethren even now coming after them?
Disappointment at their failure filled her mind for a
moment but was thrust rudely aside as another flash of
lightning tore through the sky. It was almost overhead
now, seeming to take a malevolent pleasure in playing

with them and spoiling their plans.

'Charis! Come on. We don't want them to catch us
and find out who we are.' Rafe came and took hold of
her hand, urging her along until they were over the
ridge of the hill. 'We'll have a rest when we've put
some distance between us,' he said, his mouth close to
her ear because of the thunder.

She nodded and hurried along beside him. Even
though the storm was raging it was still unbearably
hot and she was soon panting for breath, her tongue
dry in her throat. If only it would rain! Even that would
be welcome now. Another great crash of thunder
sounded above them, so loud and so close that it shook
the ground they were walking on. Charis gave a hastily
stifled whimper of fright, but she couldn't stop her
hand jerking in Rafe's. He turned to look at her, his
hand squeezing hers reassuringly. They came to the
stile leading to the public footpath and he helped her
to climb over. As he did so, the first spots of rain began
to fall. Those first few minutes were heavenly, cooling
her hot skin and taking the tension out of the air as the
thunder and lightning gradually moved away.

But as the storm went away, so the rain that came in
its aftermath increased; great pelting drops that stung
as they landed and soon soaked them to the skin. Rafe
looked round and pointed to a group of trees and they
ran to shelter under their cover.

'What about the storm?' Charis gasped as they
reached them. 'Will we be safe under the trees?'

'I should think it's far enough away now.' He drew
her close up to the trunk of a large oak tree and, as his
hand touched her bare arm, he said, concern in his
voice, 'You're shivering.'

'It's nothing.' She pushed the wet hair back off her face and folded her arms in a vain attempt to stop her teeth chattering.

'Have you got anything to wear in here?' he demanded, drawing the rucksack off his shoulder.

'There's a sweater and a cagoule, I could put those on.'

'Not on top of that wet suntop,' he told her tersely. 'Take it off and dry yourself as best you can.'

'Oh, but I can't. I haven't got . . .' She broke off in confusion, embarrassed at the thought of telling him she wasn't wearing a bra.

'If you're trying to tell me that you haven't got anything on underneath, it really isn't necessary. I can see that for myself,' Rafe told her dryly, his eyes on her chest.

Charis followed his eyes down and blushed. The cold had made her breasts harden and the wet, soft material of her top moulded them like a second skin.

Instinctively her hands went up to cover herself, but Rafe said, 'Don't be silly,' and pulled them down again.

His fingers fumbled with the hem of her top and then he was slowly pulling it up and over her head, taking it off completely. His eyes rested for long seconds on her breasts, then he rolled the top up into a ball and gently began to pat her dry.

Charis was very aware of the sound of the rain among the leaves, of the touch of the cloth on her skin, of the pressure of the other hand where he rested it on her waist, but she couldn't speak, couldn't move, could only gaze at his face as he concentrated on what he was doing. When he'd finished his eyes came up and met hers, then, very deliberately, he kissed her on the mouth, then bent his head and kissed each breast.

Her body jerked and she said his name on a gasping breath. Her eyes closed in pleasure, in expectation, but then she felt the dry sweater being pulled over her head and knew that it was over. As Rafe pulled the sweater down, she raised a trembling hand to lift her wet hair out of the neck. She searched his face, but his eyes were shadowed now and for a moment she almost believed that it had never happened, but then she felt the wool of the sweater rubbing against her bare breasts where his mouth had touched her and her body trembled again.

He gave her the cagoule and she slipped it on. He grinned at her, his manner apparently quite normal, and said, 'That was quite something you did back there—jumping on that chap just as he was about to hit me. If you hadn't he'd have knocked me cold.'

'I saw him come out and realised you couldn't see him,' Charis explained. 'I couldn't think of anything else to do.'

'It was a very brave thing to do. You're quite a girl.' He lifted a casual finger and ran it down her cheek. 'Remind me to tell you how grateful I am some time.' He moved to look out from the edge of the tree. 'It isn't going to let up, we'd better get going again.'

'But you'll get soaked,' Charis objected.

'No more than I am already. Don't worry about me,' he added roughly. 'I'm used to being wet.'

They walked on through the pelting rain, Rafe using the thin light of the torch to help them see their way, but it was difficult walking on the footpath in those conditions and Charis breathed a sigh of relief when they reached the road. Only about another mile to go now. But now that they had reached a level surface she became aware that Rafe was limping quite badly. She didn't dare say anything to him, knowing how sensitive about it he was, but she guessed that the fight, together with their scramble over the wall and the long walk, had overtired him.

'How far did you move the car?' he asked her after a while, the strain sounding in his voice.

'Not far. Just round the bend from where we pretended to break down. I was afraid to go farther than that.'

'You did well,' he told her. 'I was having kittens in case you blurted out that you couldn't drive.'

Charis turned her head and saw that he was smiling at her. He was probably in pain and definitely very tired, longing to rest his injured leg, and yet he could still smile, still take care of her and encourage her as he hurried her out of danger. She hated to think what the members of the sect might have done to him if they'd caught him, but she knew that his indomitable courage would have carried him through and he would never have told them who he was working for. Of that much about him she was absolutely certain, but as for the way he had kissed her back there, and the other two times, there Charis was completely, hopelessly lost. She had no idea what his intentions were towards her, or even whether he had any intentions at all. Whether he'd kissed her just on the spur of the moment or deliberately. But what she wondered about most of all was whether he would do it again.

CHAPTER SIX

As they came within sight of the place where she had left the car, Charis went to hurry towards it, but Rafe held her back and drew her into the trees that lined the road.

'Wait here,' he ordered. 'They might have seen the car and guessed it was ours. I'll check it out.'

He gave her the rope and knapsack and melted into the darkness. Charis waited as patiently as she could, but she was very tired now and, although the top half of her was dry, her jeans were soaked through and clung wet and cold to her legs. Rafe came back about ten minutes later, suddenly appearing and making her jerk with fright.

'It's all clear. Let's go.'

Charis climbed thankfully into the car and leaned back in the seat, longing to give way to the waves of tiredness that swept over her.

'What time is it? I forgot to wind my watch up,' she asked him as they drove back to Gloucester.

Rafe glanced at the complicated-looking quartz job on his wrist. 'Almost three,' he told her.

Something in his voice made her look at him anxiously, but it was too dark to see his face properly, she could only see his knuckles showing white as they gripped the wheel. Once he put his hand up to rub his eyes and the car swerved. He straightened it immediately and muttered, 'Sorry, must be tireder than I thought.'

When they pulled up safely in the hotel car park, Charis breathed another sigh of thankfulness; not for herself but for Rafe.

'Leave the things, I'll sort them out tomorrow,' he said as he switched off the engine.

His voice sounded slurred with exhaustion and Charis would have liked to take his arm and help him as he walked unsteadily to the entrance, but she had learnt better than that. A dim bulb still burned in the hallway as they quietly let themselves in and softly began to climb the stairs. Luckily they were carpeted and didn't creak very much. Rafe went first, holding on to the white-painted banisters, putting much of his weight on them as he went slowly up. Charis followed him, looking forward to drying her hair and taking off her wet jeans, and for a couple of minutes it didn't penetrate her mind that the dark splashes on the piece of white-painted stair between the carpet and the banister were blood. When it did she stood stock still with shock, her eyes following Rafe and only now seeing the darker stain below the knee of his left leg, a stain that dripped bright red every time he heavily lifted his leg.

Oh, God, he's torn open his wound! For a minute that was all she could think of as she stood frozen halfway up the stairs, but then Rafe began to turn to look back at her and she hastily caught him up. They reached her room first and she just gave him a quick nod and went inside. Picking up a box of tissues, Charis waited until she heard Rafe's door shut, then ran lightly back downstairs to the entrance and retraced their footsteps, carefully wiping away the bloodstains. Fortunately the carpet was a dark-coloured one and they didn't show, and those on the stairs were still wet and easily wiped away.

When she had done, Charis went back to her room and changed into pyjamas and a dressing-gown, then hesitated for only a moment before picking up the few first-aid things she had with her and taking them along to Rafe's room.

She scratched gently at his door, but it was a few moments before he opened it. She didn't give him a chance to speak but immediately slipped inside. He was still wearing his jeans but had taken off his shoes and sweater, and his shirt was undone and loose as if he was just about to take it off. Charis looked swiftly at his face and saw that it was grey, his mouth set into a pinched line.

'What do you want?' he demanded harshly.

'You know why I'm here.'

'Do I?' His eyebrows rose. 'Well, much as I'm flattered, I hardly think tonight is the right one to consummate . . .'

'Oh, shut up!' Charis said fiercely, startling him into silence. 'You know darn well I'm here because your leg's bleeding.' He began to frown, but she took no notice and held out the things she had brought. 'It's not much, but I've got a bandage and some lint.'

'All right. Thanks.' He took them from her and turned away dismissively. 'What are you waiting for?' he added gratingly when she made no move to go.

'To look at your leg, of course.'

His mouth twisted into a sneer. 'I never met a woman yet who didn't fancy herself as some sort of Florence Nightingale whenever a man scratched himself.'

'I'd hardly call it a scratch; you were dripping blood all the way up the stairs. Oh, don't worry, I went down and cleaned it up,' she added at the swift look of alarm in his eyes.

He stared at her for a moment, the grim look still in his eyes, then he said, 'Look, I appreciate what you've done, but I can manage on my own.'

Charis could have hit him. 'Oh, for heaven's sake,' she exclaimed angrily, 'why won't you let me help you? Is it some stupid point of honour or something, never to admit that you're hurt?'

'Of course not. I just don't need anyone's help. I can manage alone,' he answered curtly.

Hotly Charis retorted, 'Where does need or being able to manage come into it? If it was the other way round would you just walk away and leave me to cope alone? Well, would you?'

His jaw tightened and he glared down at her for a long moment, then looked away. 'You don't understand.'

'Possibly not.' She pointed to the little pool of blood on the lino that had trickled down his ankle. 'But in the meantime you're bleeding all over the floor. Rafe, I'm not squeamish about the sight of blood. I won't faint or anything, if that's what you're afraid of,' she added, looking at him.

He hesitated, said, 'It isn't that,' and stopped.

'Oh, really! Are you going to take your trousers off or do you want me to do it for you?'

To her surprise he laughed, although it was a dry, rather mirthless one. 'That's the best offer I've had all day. And it seems I have no choice.'

He unzipped his jeans and pulled them halfway, then sat on the bed as he took his legs out. First his right, then his left. Charis wasn't quite sure what she'd expected; a new scar that had torn open and was bleeding at the most. But never, never the ghastly mess that his leg was in. It wasn't just the blood that ran from a jagged tear just below the knee; that was the least of it. His whole leg from just about three inches above the knee to five inches below it was a mass of bright-red scar tissue, of the neat holes where dozens of stitches had been put in to hold the cicatrices, and it was a strange shape where part of the calf muscle had been completely torn away.

Almost she let her feelings show in her face, but she knew that he was watching her closely, waiting for the first sign of revulsion, and somehow she managed to keep the shock and horror out of her eyes, to school her face into impassivity as she gently bathed his leg. As she did so, she saw that she had been wrong, his wound, or rather one of his many wounds, hadn't opened up, but he had an uneven jagged cut lower down on his shin. When she had finished bandaging it up, she sat back on her heels, her face rather white.

'How did it happen?'

He chose to be obtuse. 'I must have caught it on the barbed wire as we came over the wall.'

'I see.' She got quickly to her feet and picked up his jeans from the floor, took them over to the sink and began to rinse the blood out of them. 'I'll just rinse these and you can hang them out to dry tomorrow. Then I'll leave you in peace; you must be very tired.'

He came up behind her and put his hands on her shoulders. 'Charis, don't.'

'Don't rinse your jeans, d'you mean?'

'No,' he said roughly, turning her round to face him.

'I mean stop putting on this martyred act. It's—it's something I don't enjoy talking about.'

'No, of course not.' Her chin came up and she stepped towards the door.

Rafe swore and caught her wrist, hurting her, and Charis had to stifle the wince of pain. He was immediately contrite.

'I'm sorry, I didn't mean to hurt you.'

He let go of her wrist and she stood for a minute looking down at the red marks he had made on her white skin, then said tiredly, 'I must be getting back to my room. Goodnight.'

'Goodnight—and thanks.'

She turned at the door and looked at him. 'For what? Forcing you to let me bandage you up?' She gave a tired smile. 'You were right, I would have done better to leave you alone.'

'Charis . . .'

'Goodnight, Rafe.' She turned and quietly let herself out of the door and crept back to her own room.

She was so tired that she expected to fall asleep the moment her head touched the pillow, but she kept remembering the terrible wound on Rafe's leg. He said he'd been in an accident, and she supposed that was possible, but if so, why was he reluctant to tell her about it? Heaven knows car accidents were, unfortunately, commonplace enough nowadays. Unless someone had been with him, someone he loved, and he had been responsible. That might account for his reserve, the bitterness that sometimes showed in his face.

And she had been a fool to expect him to give her his confidence. After all, they had only know each other just over a week, even though they had been in close company most of that time, much closer than in the normal course of events. And the fact that he had kissed her a couple of times obviously didn't mean a thing; not to a man like Rafe. He had more than likely made love to dozens of women in the past and had probably only kissed her because—because she was there, she supposed. They were just business partners, that was all, and once they'd got Jane out and she'd paid him, they would part and never see each other again. She had had no right to expect him to confide in her, none whatsoever.

It seemed as if she had been asleep for no time at all when Charis was woken in the morning by an urgent knock on her door. She yawned and tried to go back to sleep, but the knocking came again, louder this time. Sleepily she sat up.

'Who—who is it?' she muttered, yawning again.

'Rafe. Let me in.'

'Just a minute.' She groped for her dressing-gown and then noticed the time. Only six o'clock—and she hadn't got to bed until nearly four!

Opening the door, she moaned protestingly, 'Rafe, do you know the time?' But he quickly pushed past her and closed the door again. One look at his tense face and she was wide awake. 'What is it? What's happened? Is it your leg?'

'No.' He put his hands on her shoulders and seemed, strangely for him, to have difficulty in finding the right words, then he said, 'Charis, I'm afraid we have a problem. After you'd gone last night I took the things out of the pockets of my jeans and I found that the note you wrote to Jane was missing. It must have fallen out when I was having the set-to with the chap who tried to bash me over the head.'

Charis tried to turn her tired brain to grappling with this new development. 'You mean they'll know it was me?'

'Yes, but don't you see?' Rafe demanded impatiently. 'What's more important, they'll know it was Jane we were trying to reach. And they might think it too dangerous to keep her at the Hall when we know she's there, and so move her to another commune or even back to the headquarters in Bristol.'

'Oh, no!' Charis stared at him in horror. 'Then we'd have to start searching for her all over again!'

'Quite. That's why we've got to get moving—now.'

'But—but they might not find the note,' Charis objected, grabbing at straws.

'Possibly not, but as we were quite close to the house at the time, and the note was written on white paper, it's more than likely that it would be spotted pretty quickly. In any case, it's not a risk I'd want to take. Would you?'

'No. No, of course not.' She tried to concentrate. 'What do you want me to do?'

'Get dressed as quickly as you can. I'll wait for you in the car.'

She joined him in just over ten minutes, wearing a denim skirt and blouse with a jacket over the top. She had washed in cold water to wake herself up and was more alert now, but there were tell-tale smudges of shadow around her eyes. Rafe, in contrast, looked brisk and fully with-it, as if he'd had at least twelve hours' solid sleep instead of what could only have been an hour at the most, and that after a long walk with a cut leg, not to mention the blow on his shoulder.

He glanced at her approvingly when she joined him so quickly, but Charis returned the look rather resentfully. 'You don't looked tired at all.'

He grinned. 'You learn to manage without sleep at times in the Army.'

'Until I met you I always thought that I'd had an all-round education, but now I see that it was sadly lacking in some very vital aspects,' Charis commented tartly.

'In that case it will give me great pleasure to fill the gaps,' Rafe answered smoothly. 'But right now we have a job to do.' Opening up the map he had in his hands, he pointed to the Hall, his voice purposeful. 'There are four places we know of that they could move her to: to the farm, to Bristol, or to either of their other communes near Chippenham and in the Wye Valley. Of course they may have other places we don't know about, but I think for the moment we'll concentrate on those four and hope they'll take her to one of them.'

'But how can we possibly watch all four?' Charis asked unhappily.

'We can't. But I think we can eliminate the farm from our list; that's much more open and therefore easier for anyone who wanted to snatch one of the inmates, or for them to run away. So I think that's out. Which leaves Bristol and Chippenham to the south and Ledbury in the Wye Valley to the north. Now,' he went on, his finger tracing the route along the map, 'if they take her south they'll have to come this way, through Cirencester, and they'll have to pass this roundabout, where I intend to station myself to look out for them. If they go north to Ledbury, their most direct route is up here, bypassing Gloucester. There are

other routes they can take, but we'll just have to hope
it's this one.

'Am I going to watch that?'

'Yes. With any luck we'll be able to find somewhere
where you can watch in comfort.' He glanced at his
watch. 'We'd better get going. If they've found that
note they might move her immediately to try and fool us.'

After driving along the northern road for a few miles
they found the ideal place, a small café with a large
window looking out over the road. The only thing was,
it didn't open until eight.

'I'll have to leave you, I'm afraid,' Rafe told her.
'We'll use the hotel as a base. If you see their van
phone and leave a message for me to come and collect
you. I'll check with them as often as I can during the
course of the day. You needn't bother to phone to
check whether I've seen them, because if I do I'll
follow them and then come back for you. And if anyone
tries to make a pass at you in the café yell for the proprietor, okay?'

Charis nodded and gave the ghost of a smile. 'Okay.'

He put a hand up to her face and gently stroked her
cheek. 'Sweetheart, I know you're tired and hungry
and I'm sorry. But don't go to sleep, will you?'

Raising her head, she looked at him for a moment,
then quickly looked away and shook her head. 'No, I
won't go to sleep.'

She got out of the car and watched him as he turned
and accelerated back down the road. There was little
traffic about yet and he was soon out of sight. Feeling
strangely alone, Charis turned and looked around her.
The café was set back about ten yards from the road,
the last but one building in a longish row of houses

that made up a small hamlet. The very last building was a petrol station and garage about a hundred yards farther along, and this, too, looked to be still closed. Slinging her bag over her shoulder, Charis began to stroll along at the roadside to while away the time, being careful to face the traffic travelling north; not that there would be much chance of missing the Brotherhood's van with so little traffic about. If they used the van. The unpleasant thought came to her that if they were just moving Jane, it would be far more sensible for the Brotherhood to use just an ordinary car instead of the van, which was quite large in comparison. Which meant that she would have to try and peer into every car that went by and make her task a thousand times harder.

Her footsteps slowed and for the first time she became aware of the hazy sunshine that lay over the landscape like a photograph taken slightly out of focus, of the warm sweet smell of the grass after rain. She breathed it in deeply, enjoying the morning even though her mind was filled with anxiety about Jane—and about Rafe. Not that Rafe would thank her for worrying about him, she knew that, rather the opposite, but she couldn't help feeling concerned that he might have overdone it last night. She turned and walked back to the café, wondering if, by taking on the job of helping her, he was trying to prove to himself that he was completely fit again. Or perhaps he was trying to prove it to someone else, someone she knew nothing about. And it was unlikely she ever would know if he continued to be so withdrawn.

Sitting on a low wall outside the café, Charis waited until it opened at eight, then went inside to sit at a table by the window and ordered a large breakfast. She took as long as she could over it and the coffee that followed, then went outside and sat on the wall again. People came and went all the time, motorists stopping for morning coffee mainly, and several of them gave her curious looks as she sat in bright sunshine that had, fortunately, lost the closeness that had been in the air before the storm. At lunchtime she went back to her old table and ordered another meal, but by then her eyes were becoming sore with staring at the passing traffic, even wearing sunglasses didn't help very much, her eyes still felt stinging and gritty. Her head, too, began to ache and she would have given anything to just lean back in her seat and go to sleep. The meal helped for a while, but soon her head began to nod and she just had to take the risk of going out to the cloakroom to wash her face and splash cold water on her neck and arms.

The proprietor, a middle-aged man, gave her an odd look as she came out, and an even odder one when she ordered yet another coffee.

'Are you sure you're all right, miss?' he asked rather truculently. 'Not ill or anything?'

'Oh, no, I'm fine, thank you.' A blue van appeared in the road and Charis stiffened, leaning forward to watch it as it got nearer, but it was much bigger than the Brotherhood's, and she relaxed and sat back in her seat.

'Looking for someone, was you?' the man enquired.

'Well—er—yes.' She sought for an excuse. 'As a matter of fact my friend was supposed to meet me here, but his car must have broken down or something.' It was a feeble enough pretext but all she could think of when her head ached so much.

The man sniffed and didn't look too happy about it, but at least he went away and left her alone.

The sun moved slowly round in the sky until it was directly facing her, making her eyes swim as she tried to peer into every car that passed. By now she had almost given up hope, sure that the Brotherhood, even if they had found the note, had decided that Jane would be safer if they kept her at the Hall. After all, they were forewarned now and would be on the lookout for another attempt to reach her. And again, if there was no sign of Jane today what could she and Rafe do? They couldn't watch all night as well and it was quite likely that if Jane was moved at all, it would be under the cover of darkness. Despair filled her heart and she was close to tears. They had got so near, so very near, only to have everything go wrong because of the storm. If that hadn't happened they might have had Jane safely in the nursing home by now and the whole thing over with. But now everything seemed hopeless.

'You sure you're all right?'

The proprietor's gruff question made her put a quick finger up to wipe her eyes. 'Oh, yes. I'm just a bit tired, that's all.'

'You look it,' agreed the Job's comforter. 'A man, is it? The friend you're waiting for,' he added when she frowned in puzzlement.

She nodded. 'Yes, it's a man.'

'Thought as much,' he grunted. 'You got anywhere to go?'

Charis realised that he spoke with reluctant concern and hastened to reassure him. 'Thank you, but I'm all right, really.'

'Hmph,' he muttered disbelievingly. 'Well, we close at six.'

Looking at the clock on the wall, Charis saw that it was almost that now, and reluctantly she drained the last of her coffee; she'd lost count of how many she'd drunk today, but at least they'd helped to keep her awake. She paid her bill, one eye still on the road as she hunted in her purse for the money, and then went outside to take up her now familiar perch on the wall again. It was cooler now and Charis slipped on her jacket. A couple of people who must have been working in the kitchen of the café came out, got into a car and joined the steady stream of traffic; people coming home from work in Gloucester or holidaymakers heading back to their hotels for dinner, Charis guessed. The sun was lower in the sky now and reflected off the windscreens of the oncoming cars, blinding her, making her frown and flinch away, so that she had great difficulty in seeing the occupants at all. She felt very close to tears, knowing that Jane might already have passed her and she'd not seen her. Her only hope now was that Rafe would have been luckier and that he would soon come along and pick her up.

But time dragged on and he didn't come. The traffic thinned out and the sun sank behind some tall trees, giving her eyes some relief at last. Leaning her head back against the wall of the café, Charis relaxed, her eyes heavy, then jerked awake as her head began to nod. Remembering her promise to Rafe, she sat upright, determined to keep awake, but her head was getting heavier by the minute. It was almost dusk when the blue van came along, and by that time she was digging her nails hard into her arms to try and keep herself awake, was concentrating so much on it that she hardly saw the van until it was almost up to her. But then she forced her eyes to open and recognition came. And with it the realisation that a girl was sitting by the window, looking uninterestedly out.

Charis' breath caught in her throat and she sat up, staring. The girl was blonde and pretty, her eyes settled on Charis and a slight frown came into them, the puzzled sort of look that people get when they think they recognise someone but aren't quite sure who they are. Then the van was past.

Charis found that she'd got to her feet and had started to run after the van, but stopped abruptly as she realised it was a foolish thing to do. She stood at the edge of the road, gazing after it, and tears began to run down her cheeks and suddenly she was crying. She'd seen her sister! For the first time in three months she knew that Jane was at least alive and well. Slowly she turned and picked up her bag which she had dropped in her excitement. She tried to think what she had to do next, but all the pent-up anxieties of the last few months, the long, worrying day on top of a virtually sleepless night, and above everything else that vacant look she had seen on Jane's face, all caught up with her and she just put her hands up to her face and stood and sobbed.

It was a while before she could pull herself together enough to think straight, and it suddenly came to her what a ridiculous figure she must look, standing in the kerb crying her eyes out. That thought made her laugh a little and she wiped her eyes, blew her nose rather determinedly and set off to look for a phone box. She found one outside the small sub-post office-cum general store in the village and left a carefully-worded message at the hotel for Rafe, telling him where she was.

Over an hour later he found her lying curled up on a wooden bench outside the shop, her head pillowed on her bag, fast alseep. He didn't wake her at once, but stood gazing down at her, a strange look on his face, then he bent and gently flicked a finger against her cheek. Somewhat to his surprise, she woke at once and sat up, giving him a weary smile.

'I saw her, Rafe—I actually saw her!'

'Good girl! Now, let's get you home.'

He helped her to her feet and put his arm round her as he walked her over to the car.

Charis sat back thankfully in the seat, her eyes already starting to close again.

'Was she in the van?' Rafe asked as he got in beside her.

'Yes.'

'Were there any other passengers?'

Her forehead creased into a frown as Charis tried to remember. 'I don't know—I only saw Jane. I mean, there *might* have been other passengers, but I just didn't see them; I only saw Jane.'

'Okay. Don't worry about it.' Leaning forward to look at her more closely, he added, 'You've been crying.'

'Yes, I suppose I have. Does it show? It's only because I was so tired.' She gave him a heavy-eyed smile. 'You must be exhausted, you've had even less sleep than I have, besides doing all the driving. Yet you don't look it.'

He shrugged. 'I'm stronger than you are. I'm a man.'

Turning towards him, Charis said softly, 'Yes, I know.' Her eyes large in her face, she reached up and put a hand on his shoulder. 'Rafe?'

'Yes.'

She didn't speak, just moved her hand so that her fingers gently traced the outline of his jaw. The last rays of the sunset lit her face, showing him her eyes, wide and shadowed and her lips parted sensuously.

His voice sounding strange, Rafe said roughly, 'Tell me what you want.'

'I want . . .' Her finger found his mouth and, delicate as a butterfly's wing, travelled the length of his lips. 'I want you to kiss me,' she whispered hardly aloud, almost to herself.

For a long moment he didn't move, just looked down at her as if he was considering the idea, then slowly reached out and put a hand behind her neck, drawing her towards him. He kissed her almost brutally, his mouth hard and without tenderness, and as he felt her lips soft and yielding, beneath his own, he made a noise deep in his throat and became more compulsive, more demanding. Then he drew away suddenly, his breathing unsteady.

'It's getting late,' he said abruptly. 'I'm taking you home.'

Charis stared up at him, her eyes wide and frightened, but then exhaustion overcame her and she leaned her head on his shoulder. She was asleep within seconds, so that she didn't see the long, frowning look Rafe gave her before he started the car and drove away.

CHAPTER SEVEN

CHARIS couldn't remember getting undressed and going to bed, but she supposed she must have done; she was certainly wearing only her nightdress when Rafe banged on her door to wake her the next morning. Looking at her watch, she saw that it was after eight o'clock and got quickly out of bed.

'Just a minute!' she called out as she began to put on her dressing-gown.

'It's all right, you needn't bother to come to the door. I just wanted to remind you to pack. We'll be leaving here today, so be down as soon as possible, would you, please?'

Even through the thickness of the door it sounded like an order, and for a moment Charis was puzzled by his tone, by his lack of courtesy in even wishing her good morning, but then she shrugged it off; calling out pleasantries for anyone who might be passing to hear was hardly in Rafe's line.

She hurried to obey him, washing and dressing quickly and packing her suitcase, glad that she hadn't brought very much with her. Picking up the sun-top she'd been wearing on the night of the storm, Charis found that it was still slightly damp; there had been no time yesterday to lay it out to dry. Seeing it made her recall vividly how Rafe had taken it off and dried her with it, his gentleness, and, most vividly of all, the way he had kissed her afterwards, first on her mouth, then on her breasts. Her hands began to shake a little as she carefully folded the shirt and put it in a plastic bag before placing it in the suitcase. How strange to think that that was only two days ago; so much time seemed to have passed since then, a whole, long day in which she and Rafe had been apart and she hadn't been able to talk to him, to look at him and try and guess what he was feeling under that enigmatic exterior. There had only been those few minutes in the car after he had picked her up, when he had kissed her. And she had been so tired, almost asleep, that it could have been a dream. But she knew that it wasn't, because it sent an odd shiver of uneasiness through her now that she thought of it. For a moment she couldn't think why, but then she remembered that Rafe had always been gentle before, but not last night. Last night he had kissed her with a fervour that had frightened and startled her. Compared to that, his earlier kisses now seemed more like friendly pecks. And she could find no reason for the abrupt change, nor for the way he had stopped kissing her so suddenly. Only one thing was sure, now she could no longer go on pretending that their relationship was merely a casual one; up to the moment he kissed her last night it could have gone on and ended that way, but not any more. Some time she was going to have to try and sort out her own feelings. But not now, now there wasn't time.

Charis put the last few things into her case, closed it and carried that and her bag downstairs to the lobby. She found Rafe sitting at a table in the breakfast room, reading the morning paper over a cup of coffee. There were several other people in the room and the tables were crowded quite close together, so there wasn't much opportunity to talk, not that Rafe showed much inclination to; he merely nodded to her when she sat down opposite him and then went back to his paper. Charis smiled slightly, because the action seemed so typical of the popular comedy concept of a husband and wife situation, but then she hastily pushed the thought aside, afraid of it.

The hotel might have been shabby and second-rate, but there was nothing wrong with the service; Charis had only been sitting down for a couple of minutes before a waitress came up to take her order. And the breakfast was good, too. There was a choice of cereal or porridge to start with and she followed this up with a large helping of scrambled egg and bacon that was cooked just right. When she got to the coffee and toast stage, Rafe surfaced and folded the paper. Standing up, he said, 'I'll go and pay the bill and put the stuff in the car. Did you bring your case down?'

'Yes, it's in the lobby.'

He nodded and went away, leaving Charis to finish her coffee. He seemed to want to leave as soon as possible and she tried to hurry, but the coffee was too hot. She wondered what he had in mind for them today and where they would be going. Somewhere near the new commune that Jane had been taken to, presumably. It was the first time that she'd thought of her sister that day, and she realised it with feelings of surprise and guilt. She had been so busy thinking about Rafe that Jane, the sole reason for them being together here, hadn't entered her mind.

Finishing her coffee, Charis walked out into the lobby with a rather preoccupied frown on her face. The middle-aged receptionist was on duty again and bade her goodbye with a puzzled and slightly disappointed look, as if Charis and Rafe had let her down by sticking to their own bedrooms during their stay, when she'd been certain that they would end up together. Rafe was sitting in the car smoking a cigarette as he waited for her. He ground it out as soon as she got in; she'd noticed that he never smoked while he was driving.

'All set?' She nodded and he passed her the map. 'We're making for Ledbury.'

Correctly interpreting this as an order to navigate, Charis obediently opened the map to work out the route. The first part of the way was the same as that they had covered the previous day, and it gave Charis a strange feeling as they passed the café where she had spent so many long, tired hours. She wondered whether the proprietor had given her another thought, or whether he had dismissed her as just another troublesome holidaymaker; he probably had enough problems of his own without worrying about every stranger who came into his premises and sat gazing out of the window. No, he had probably forgotten her already, their lives had touched very briefly through force of circumstance, just as circumstance had brought her in contact with Rafe.

She stole a glance at him, but he was looking directly ahead, concentrating on the road, although there was no great need to, for the road was fairly straight and there wasn't a great deal of traffic. She opened her mouth to make a remark, to start a conversation, but there was something about the set of his chin and the grimness of his mouth that made her change her mind and the words died in her throat.

Today wasn't the day for idle conversation.

As they approached the little market town of Ledbury, the traffic became much denser and there were frequent hold-ups. The reason for this they found when Rafe pulled into a garage for petrol and the attendant told them that it was carnival week in the town, that there was a big fair there, and also a procession due to go through the town centre that day.

Rafe brought his hand down upon the steering-wheel in frustration. 'Just my luck!' he exclaimed in annoyance.

Charis looked at him and said quietly. '*Your* luck?'

He glanced at her briefly. 'All right, *our* luck, then. You realise this means we're going to have a hell of a job finding somewhere to stay? I was hoping that we could get settled in somewhere and I could drive out and have a look at this new commune today.'

'You think it necessary to hurry that much? Wouldn't it be better to wait a couple of days in case they're still on their guard?'

'No, it wouldn't,' Rafe replied so curtly that it was almost rude. 'A couple of days isn't going to make any difference; it would take at least a couple of months before the Brotherhood might begin to relax their watch over Jane again. And we have the slight advantage that they might believe that we still expect her to be at the Hall, that we might not know about this place. So it might take them by surprise if we have a go at getting her out as soon as possible. And anyway,' he added as he restarted the car, 'I don't want to waste a day longer on this job than I have to.'

His voice had been deliberately harsh as he said that last sentence and Charis turned to look out of her window, biting her lip. There could be no doubt of it now; he was angry with her and wanted the whole thing over and done with, although she couldn't think what she'd done to make him feel that way. She sat silently in the car, trying to puzzle it out. Surely it wasn't because she had insisted on tending his leg and had seen his scars? That had been two days ago and although they hadn't seen much of each other yesterday morning, he hadn't been at all angry, quite the opposite in fact, she thought as she remembered the way he'd gently touched her face as he had left her outside the café. He had even called her sweetheart; not that that meant anything, of course, it was just a word he used, like a nickname. But it was certainly a lot different from his manner towards her today. Which again brought her back to that kiss last night. There had been anger in that, too. Then she remembered that she had asked him to kiss her, and a rush of shame ran through her. Could *that* be why he was so angry? Because she'd asked? Or because he'd complied? But surely that wasn't such a terrible thing to do? After all, this was the twentieth century, not the eighteenth! Or maybe Rafe was the type who didn't like having the initiative taken out of his hands. Maybe he didn't like the type of girl who would take it. She looked at him again as he tapped impatiently on the steering-wheel, waiting for yet another jam to clear, his chin jutting forward angrily. His moods seemed to be as mercurial as the electric storm two nights ago and his anger just as cruel.

They eventually managed to park the car in a field that was being used as a temporary car park some way outside Ledbury and walked back. The town seemed

to mainly comprise one long High Street with shops
on either side and interesting black and white timbered
houses and inns. The pavements were already quite
thickly lined with people who were waiting to watch
the procession, although this wasn't due to start for an
hour yet. Luckily the pavements were quite wide and
they were able to make their way behind the crowd
down towards the centre of the High Street where the
road opened out to encompass a cobbled area on which
stood the old Market Hall, an elevated building, sup-
ported on a great many pillars, under which the market
stalls still stood one day a week, just as they had stood
since the place was built hundreds of years ago. There
were some stalls there today, selling mostly soft drinks
and snacks, and there was a notice at the foot of the
stairs leading up to the closed-in upper floor advertising an arts and crafts exhibition which was on until the
end of the carnival week.

Charis would have liked to visit the exhibition, but
didn't dare suggest it as she followed Rafe across the
road to the Tourist Information Office.

Here they had no luck at all in finding any accom-
modation. It seemed that the town was full right up,
there wasn't even one room available in any of the local
houses that were offering bed and breakfast, let alone
two. It was an annoyance made only easier by the girl
in the office, who seemed genuinely sorry that she was
unable to help them and suggested they try Great
Malvern, the largest town in the area, where there were
far more hotels than in a small place like Ledbury.

'It looks as if we'll have to do as she suggests,' Rafe
said ruefully as they came out into the sunshine again.
'Let's hope we're luckier there.'

They were, eventually. But it took nearly the whole day, travelling round the three towns that surrounded the rolling Malvern Hills, before they found somewhere, and then it was only a caravan. It had been offered to them by the Tourist Bureau in Great Malvern earlier on in the day, but Rafe had immediately rejected it out of hand and they had gone on to the next town. But here again there was the same story: the school holidays had started, it was carnival time, everywhere was already booked. Only when it was obvious that there was nothing else available and it began to get late did Rafe concede defeat and they drove back to Great Malvern and hired the trailer.

Charis had kept quiet all day, wisely not pushing Rafe or making any suggestions, knowing that the frustration of not being able to find anywhere must only be fuelling his anger. She wasn't all that keen on the idea of a trailer herself, but she was getting tired and definitely fed up with driving around trying to find somewhere and would happily have settled for a tent rather than look any farther.

The trailer wasn't on a site, but stood by itself at the bottom of a garden belonging to a largish cottage, but screened from it by a trellis covered with sweet-smelling rambling roses. It was approached by a lane that led down the side of the property and had its own parking space alongside, so that it was completely self-contained from the cottage. Never having stayed in a trailer before, Chris had no idea what to expect and was pleasantly surprised when Rafe let them in with a key he had collected from the cottage, and she found that the trailer was quite large and new, and immaculately clean. Her tiredness forgotten, she opened the curtains to let in the fading sunlight and exclaimed with delight as she discovered the compact cooker and sink.

'Good heavens, there's a fridge, too. Look!' she exclaimed as she pulled open drawers and cupboards. 'It's got everything you need. And this must be the bedroom.' She opened the rear door and saw the two bunks, then frowned. 'I thought the woman at the Bureau said it slept four?'

'The table probably folds down and you use the seats on either side to make a double bunk,' Rafe told her, indicating the dining table with its cushioned seats.

Charis laughed. 'How ingenious! I'd no idea they were so compact. It's great, isn't it?'

'Oh, sure. Home from home,' Rafe agreed sneeringly.

The smile faded and Charis turned to pick up the bag of groceries they had bought on the way. Her back to him, she said, 'I'll cook the steaks. Could you check that the gas is turned on, please?'

He did so and then went into the tiny bathroom to shower and change. The meal was ready by the time he came out and he took his place opposite her. The table wasn't very wide and their knees touched beneath it. Charis hastily moved hers out of the way.

They had bought a bottle of wine and she had it standing on the table ready with a corkscrew that she had found in a drawer.

'You're very efficient,' he remarked sardonically as he picked up the corkscrew and opened the bottle. He did so deftly, obviously having done the job dozens of times before, and poured some of the blood red liquid into their glasses. 'Cheers.' He lifted his glass to toast her, but there was no warmth in his tone.

'Cheers.' She returned the toast and sipped the wine experimentally, then let it roll to the back of her palate. It was a wine she hadn't tried before, but she liked it; it was dry, but not so dry that it made her cringe.

Rafe watched her and said, parodying a waiter but with sarcasm in his voice, 'I trust the wine is to your liking, madam?'

Charis flushed a little. 'Yes, thank you, it's fine.'

'You being a connoisseur, of course?'

'No, I'm not,' she replied steadily. 'And obviously I'm not in your class. But I like drinking wine and I've read a bit about it. And even though I can't tell you which slope of which particular vineyard a wine comes from, I can at least tell whether or not I like it. Maybe,' she added tartly, 'when I'm as old as you my palate will be more discerning!'

Rafe's fingers tightened on his glass and his eyes narrowed. For a moment she thought that he was about to make an angry retort, but then his hand relaxed and he said coolly, 'I stand rebuked.'

He turned his attention on his meal, but there was a tension between them that grew by the minute. To break it, Charis said brightly, 'Maybe taking this trailer wasn't such a bad idea after all. I mean, it's quite private, so no one would see us come and go if we wanted to visit the commune at night. No one to be curious if we go out early in the morning and don't come back till late.' Warming to her theme, she added, 'When we get Jane out we could even bring her back here.' She waited for him to make some reply, but when he didn't, she persisted, 'Don't you think those are advantages over a hotel?'

His eyes came up slowly to meet hers; they were very blue, as blue as the summer sky. 'Maybe they are. But taking this trailer was a damn fool idea and we're moving out the minute we can get a vacancy in a hotel!' He set down his glass with a snap and stood up.

Charis stared up at him, her face pale, and said with a shaky laugh, 'I hadn't realised my cooking was quite that bad!' Then, slowly, 'Have I—offended you in some way, Rafe?'

He looked down at her for a long moment without answering, then he turned his head a little and said, 'I'm going to drive to a pub for a drink. Do you want to come?'

'Do you want me to?'

'For God's sake, woman!' he exclaimed exasperatedly. 'Do you want to come or don't you?'

'Yes, of course I want to,' Charis retorted sharply. 'I just thought that you might want to be alone. Everyone needs to be alone sometimes.'

Her reply seemed to startle him. He stared at her for a moment, then gave a sort of sigh and said, 'Why don't you get ready?'

It was still quite early in the evening when they left, the sky still shot with the deep gold of sunset as it sank behind the hills. The scenery was beautiful; Charis thought it one of the most beautiful parts of England that she had ever visited. It wasn't spectacular scenery; there were no grey, rocky heights or tumbling rivers, just green hills and pleasant valleys, covered with the green of trees and the yellow of fields of crops. The air was warm and gentle and the villages nestled peacefully and confidently in that pleasant land. Charis gazed wistfully out of the car window and wished with all her heart that she could be a part of one of these small communities, look out of a window every waking morning to this loveliest of landscapes, instead of being a minute, nameless face in the London anthill.

Rafe drove the ten miles back to Ledbury where it was much easier to find a parking space now that the day trippers had all gone. The fair, though, was still going strong; they could hear the noise of it through the open latticed-windows of the pub they chose just off the High Street. It was an old pub with a deep inglenooked fireplace, and a wooden-beamed ceiling so low that Rafe had to duck when he passed under them as he brought their drinks to their table.

Charis smiled at him. 'Being tall has its disadvantages.'

He nodded and sat down opposite, although there was plenty of room on the settle beside her.

For a few minutes they drank in silence, then Charis, keeping her voice as firm as she could, said, 'You didn't answer my question when we were back at the trailer.'

'Really?' His chin came up, challenging her to go on.

'Yes. I asked you if I'd offended you in any way?' Somehow she managed to say it although his eyes were now ice-cold.

Charis searched his face, waiting for a reply, but a mask had come down over his features and he looked away so that she could tell nothing from his eyes.

'Of course not.' He dismissed the question with a wave of his hand and abruptly changed the subject. 'We'd better discuss the plans for tomorrow. First I'll have to locate the commune and find out exactly what kind of place it is and how many people are living there.

From the information my journalist friend gave me before we came, it seems to be the smallest of the four, which could be to our advantage.'

'And it could hardly be less accessible than the Hall.'

'No,' Rafe agreed. 'With luck I'll be able to give the place a good look over tomorrow and work out some way of getting into it either tomorrow night or the night after. It depends on what equipment I might need.'

'You keep saying I,' Charis pointed out. 'Don't you mean we?'

'No, I don't,' he answered shortly. 'I'm doing this one alone.'

'Oh. Why?'

'Because I can get on better and quicker on my own.'

'But you don't know what you're going to do yet. And you might need help in watching the . . .'

His voice harsh, Rafe cut in, 'I don't need any help. I can manage perfectly well alone.'

'Can you?' Her face flushed, Charis added acidly, 'I seem to remember that you were glad enough of my help when that man attacked you at the Hall.' His face tautened and Charis, realising that they were quarrelling, looked away wretchedly. She started to say, 'I'm sorry . . .' but Rafe interrupted her.

'You're quite right; I was glad of your help. But it's because of that that I'm not taking you with me this time. They've seen you. They know who you are. If they caught a glimpse of you near the commune they would know that we'd traced Jane here and they'd move her. Do you want that to happen?'

He spoke brusquely, almost insolently, as if she had been a fool not to think of it for herself. She looked at him miserably, not knowing what she'd done or how to get their relationship back on its old footing again. Rafe took her silence for acceptance of his orders and stood up, his glass in his hand. 'I'm going over to the bar to talk to some of the locals, see if I can find out anything about the commune.'

He left her sitting at the table alone with nothing to do but look at his broad back and wonder about him. She knew so little about him really. He had told her nothing about his background, his family. All she knew was that he had been invalided out of the Army and that he wasn't married. And she hadn't even bothered to check up on the facts he had given her, which she could easily have done by consulting the Army List. No, there had been something about him that had drawn her to him and made her trust him right from the very first. And she couldn't believe that she'd been wrong. Something had happened to upset him, and he wouldn't tell her what it was. Perhaps all their activity the other night had been too much for his leg and he wouldn't admit it? But he had shown no sign of pain all day, and, even so, it would be no reason to be so rude to her.

She was still brooding about it when Rafe came back to sit with her, bringing her another drink.

'Did you find anything out?' she asked him stiltedly.

He shook his head. 'Nothing of any use. No one seems to know much about them. They don't seem to get any supplies from any of the shops in the town and none of the inmates come here at all. But I did find out more or less where it's situated.'

'Well, that's something.'

'It's about three miles north of here towards Great Malvern, so I suppose it's possible that they could go there for any supplies they need, but from what I can gather they try to grow as much of their own food as they can. The locals here seem to know nothing about their being a religious sect; they think they're just a bunch of people who've got together to form a self-sufficient community. They might not like it from the moral aspect, but on the whole they're willing to live and let live.' He finished his drink and said, 'We may as well go, if you're ready.'

It was cooler when they came out and Charis paused to put on her jacket. The sound of the fair seemed louder now as it carried on the evening air. It was a mixture of sounds that would be identifiable as that of a funfair anywhere in the world: the blatant music of an electric organ, the loud hum of the generators, the crash of the dodgem cars, and the shrill cries of laughter and fear of the people on the rides; a variety of noises that put together immediately sent a flame of excitement through the veins and drew one like a magnet towards the lights and movement.

Charis raised her head to listen, then impulsively reached out and touched Rafe's arm. 'Oh, please, can we go to the fair?'

He looked at her in surprise. 'What on earth for?'

She laughed a little exasperatedly. 'Why does anyone want to go to the fair? To go on the rides and things, of course.'

After hesitating a moment, he shrugged and spoke as if indulging a child. 'All right, if that's what you want.'

His tone had been less than enthusiastic, but Charis ignored it and turned towards the fair. It was in an open area off a side road a few hundred yards away, and her steps quickened as she neared it. They had always loved fairs, she and Jane, their parents had taken them every Easter to the big one that came to Hampstead Heath, in London. This fair, in comparison, was small, but it had all the main components: a helter-skelter, rocket ships, dodgem cars, lots of side stalls, and—most important of all—an old-fashioned roundabout with gaily painted horses prancing endlessly round and round.

Charis turned to Rafe, her face glowing. 'We must go on the roundabout first. That's always the first ride.'

She hurried up to it and climbed aboard as soon as the music stopped, choosing a really fiery-looking white horse with an impossibly long red tongue protruding from its mouth. Laughing, she looked round for Rafe, but he hadn't followed her, he was still standing a few yards away lighting a cigarette and looking bored. A wave of wretchedness filled her, swiftly followed by anger. To hell with Rafe! If he wouldn't tell her what was the matter, then there was nothing she could do about it. And she certainly wasn't going to let it spoil her enjoyment. The music started again and the roundabout began to turn, the horses lifting and falling as they began to go faster. There was a little girl on the next horse and Charis smiled and laughed with her, her face alive and happy, her fair hair blown into a silken cloud round her head. Lifting her eyes on one of the turns, she caught a glimpse of Rafe and saw that he was watching her, an arrested expression on his face, the bored look completely gone.

After the roundabout she pulled him towards the dodgem cars and insisted he join her. 'You know I can't drive,' she reminded him.

'You don't have to drive for one of those things, anyone can do it.'

'But it's much better if you can. Oh, come on, Rafe, don't be such an old fuddy-duddy!'

He shot her a darkling look but climbed into a car beside her. It was very cramped, especially with someone as big as Rafe, and Charis was squashed tight against the side of the car. Someone smashed into the side of them and jolted her so that she gave a yelp and rubbed her arm. Rafe hesitated for a moment, then lifted one arm to put it round her, steering with one hand, and it was soon obvious that he was enjoying himself as much as she was as he piloted them through the throng of demon drivers. Charis held tightly to the front of the car and laughed and called out a warning whenever another car came too close, but she felt strangely as if she was divided in two; one half of her was participating in the ride, the other half was aware of nothing but Rafe's closeness, of the hardness of his thigh against her own, of the strength of his arm around her shoulders, protecting her, of his sheer masculinity.

When the ride was over she found that her legs were shaky and stumbled so that Rafe caught her arm.

'Are you all right?'

'Yes, fine.' Charis laughed unsteadily. 'Let's go on the rocket ships next.'

He protested, but she didn't have too much difficulty

in persuading him to go with her, and even less on the caterpillar, where he again found it necessary to put his arm round her to prevent her from sliding off the seat. But he drew the line at the helter-skelter.

'You don't seriously expect me to go on that? It's for kids!'

Charis gave him a saucy look. 'I suppose you think it's beneath your dignity?'

He went to make a retort but saw the challenging look in her eyes and gave in with a grimace. 'All right, but this is the last one.'

They climbed up the inside of the unwieldy-looking structure carrying their mats, and Charis paused at the top, looking out across the fair.

'Scared?' Rafe asked, behind her.

She turned to look at him, silhouetted against the coloured lights around the dome. 'No, I'm not afraid.'

'Let's go down together, then.'

She sat in front of him between his legs, his arms holding her firmly round the waist, and they flew down, laughing and falling in a heap on the pile of rugs at the bottom.

Charis was still laughing as Rafe picked himself up and then bent to help her. He, too, was grinning and started to say something about, 'They'd never believe this in the mess . . .' but then the smile faded and an intense look came into his eyes. He pulled her to her feet and held her for a moment, his fingers gripping hard. He said her name on a low note, but then someone else came down the slide and knocked into them and the moment was past, lost. Rafe blinked and turned away, walking her towards the entrance, his face grim again.

In a forlorn attempt to recapture his former carefree mood, Charis insisted that he tried his hand at the rifle range. He did so reluctantly, but then fired fiercely at the targets as if he was destroying an enemy, and was such a good shot that the stallholder refused to let him have another turn after he'd won three prizes, one after the other. He gave her the cuddly toys she'd chosen and said, '*Now* can we go?'

They drove back through the starlit night and parked the car beside the caravan. Rafe unlocked the door and turned on the light. 'You can take the bedroom and I'll make up the bed in here,' he told her. 'Then I won't disturb you when I make an early start in the morning.'

Calmly Charis said, 'We'll both be making an early start; I'm coming with you.'

Rafe's eyes narrowed. 'We've already had this out. I'm going alone.'

'I'm coming with you, and you can't stop me.'

A dangerous look came into his face. 'Can't I?'

'No,' Charis persisted determinedly. 'Because you seem to have forgotten that I hired you, and I give the orders around here.'

'Do you, by God?' He stared at her in astonishment and growing anger. Then said grimly, 'And what if I tell you that I either go alone or I pack the whole thing in and go back to London?'

He stood glaring at her, his jaw thrust forward, certain that he had won. But Charis squared her shoulders and faced him defiantly. 'That's your privilege, of course. No one made you sign any contracts. You're free to give up the job any time you want.'

'And what about Jane?' he asked sarcastically. 'Or

have you forgotten about her?'

'No, of course I haven't. I shall go and try and get her out myself. I haven't come all this way to not go on—either with you or without you.'

Dark anger showed in his face and he caught her wrist. 'Don't try and blackmail me. You wouldn't dare to go there alone.' He shook her violently and she stumbled against him. 'Would you? Would you?' Suddenly his hands were on her shoulders, biting into her flesh. His lips were drawn back in a kind of snarl, but the anger in his face was mixed with something else, and then he pulled her hard against him, imprisoning her as his lips fastened on hers with a savage, compulsive hunger.

CHAPTER EIGHT

IT happened so suddenly that Charis was taken completely by surprise. When Rafe had started to shake her, she had automatically lifted her hands in a defensive gesture, but now she was held so tightly against him that her arms were pinned against his body and she couldn't move. Not that she tried to move; her whole attention was focussed on what he was doing to her. His lips were hard against her own, forcing her into submission, demanding a response. He kissed her so passionately that he hurt her and she made a sound of protest, but it didn't make him let up at all, if anything it only increased his urgency and he succeeded in forcing her lips apart. Charis gave a gasp and struggled to be free, jerking her head away.

For a moment they stared at each other, both hot and breathless, then Charis lifted her arms and put them round his neck and suddenly she was kissing him back, kissing him with far less skill but just as much passion and desire. Her head began to whirl, she moaned as he held her hard against him and flames of sensuality ran through her body. Her nails dug into his shoulders as his lips left hers to explore her throat, her eyes, the curves of her cheek, then fastened greedily on her mouth again.

His hands were at her clothes, slipping off her jacket, then undoing the buttons of her shirt. His hands slipped inside, found her breasts, moulding and caressing the bare flesh, and Charis groaned, her body arching towards him. Rafe lifted his head so that he could look at her, and then his lips were on her throat, her shoulder, and going on down until she gave a cry of pleasure as they found her breasts. Her body quivered as her hands gripped his shoulders and she said his name over and over again.

Slowly he straightened up, his breathing uneven, his eyes dark with need. Charis clung to him, mouth parted sensuously, aware of nothing but the hedonistic sensations he had aroused in her. She moved against him, needing, wanting him. 'Oh, Rafe,' she breathed, 'I love you!'

It was almost as if she hadn't spoken the words with her mouth, almost as if they had come from deep inside her. For a moment Rafe didn't react; but then his hands stilled on her breasts and he lifted his head from where he had been kissing her throat. He looked down at her, then his body seemed to jerk and he stepped back, his face becoming grim, remote.

At first Charis didn't realise what had happened and she moved towards him, wanting to have him hold her again, to feel his arms around her, but he pushed her away roughly. Slowly she became aware of his withdrawal and looked at him uncomprehendingly.

'Rafe?' He didn't answer, just looked at her with that closed, shut-in expression. 'What—what is it?'

For answer, he just said harshly, 'We've an early start tomorrow. You'd better go to bed.'

'But—but I don't understand.' She looked at him uncomprehendingly, then became aware that her shirt was open and her breasts exposed. With shaking fingers she covered herself, feeling suddenly ashamed of her nakedness.

'Don't you?' Rafe demanded harshly. 'Do you really not understand?'

Tremblingly she shook her head, feeling suddenly afraid.

'You said that you loved me,' he told her, making it sound like an accusation.'

'Oh!' She blushed furiously and looked away. 'Did I?'

'Oh, yes, you said it all right. And presumably you meant it?'

'Yes, I suppose I did,' she agreed slowly, then raised her head to look at him directly. 'Is that—so very wrong?'

'Wrong?' He looked at her in angry exasperation. 'It just proves what I was beginning to suspect about you. That you don't know how to play the game.'

'Game? What game?' Charis looked at him in utter bewilderment.

'The game of love, of sex—call it what you like,' he said contemptuously. 'You're not like most women who know that it's all a game; you're the old-fashioned type to whom sex means love and love means marriage.'

'Doesn't it to you?' Charis asked him, her face rather white.

'No.' He shook his head in a curt negative. 'I can't let it mean that to me.' He turned and paced the two strides which was all the room he had in the confined space. 'I *knew* we shouldn't have taken this damn trailer. I was afraid of something like this happening. I've been afraid of it ever since . . .'

He paused, and Charis, her senses suddenly acute,

finished it for him. 'Ever since I asked you to kiss me last night.'

'Yes.'

'And that's why you've been so beastly to me today, because you were afraid I was falling for you and you wanted to put me off.'

'Yes,' he agreed again, heavily.

'I see.' Her face tense, Charis turned and slid into the seat at one side of the table, her hands hidden beneath it. 'So where do we go from here?'

Rafe looked down at her with grudging admiration, grateful that she hadn't cried or made a scene. He leant back against the wall and lit a cigarette with fingers that weren't quite steady. After a few moments he said stiltedly, 'I'm sorry, it's my fault. If I'd realised earlier what kind of girl you were I'd have made sure that we stayed on a strictly business footing.'

'The women that you usually meet,' Charis said slowly, 'I suppose they all know how to play your—game?'

'Yes, of course they do,' he answered irritably. 'Otherwise . . .'

'Otherwise you'd have run a mile, afraid of being caught in the marriage trap,' Charis finished with a rather bitter smile.

'I'm a career soldier,' he snapped out. 'The Army is the only . . .' and then he broke off, remembering, and Charis' heart contracted with pity as she saw the spasm of pain that jerked across his face. Bitterly he corrected himself, 'The Army *was* all I ever wanted.'

Charis looked down at the table and they were both silent for some time, then she said in as matter-of-fact voice as she could manage, 'Will you still help me to get my sister—on the understanding that our relationship is just a temporary partnership until then, of course?'

'Yes, of course.'

'Very well.' Charis stood up and moved towards the door to the bedroom. She opened it, then paused and turned to look at him. 'I'm sorry I didn't know the rules of your game.' Adding cynically, 'I'm sure you'd have made a good teacher.'

And he could take that which way he liked, Charis thought bitterly as she closed the door behind her and leaned on it, very close to tears. But she blinked them back, knowing how thin the walls were and that he would hear. Grimly she got ready for bed and crawled into the sleeping bag, to lie awake in the darkness. She could hear Rafe moving about, making up his bed, she supposed, then the light went out, there was the sound of a door being closed, and everything was quiet. It was a very tense quiet, like that before the electric storm, and just as charged. Charis was deeply aware of his nearness and knew that he, too, must be thinking of it. He had accused her of being old-fashioned, and maybe she was, but that didn't make her feelings any the less intense, her emotions and needs any less passionate. She hadn't been out with many men, certainly none as self-assured as Rafe, and her emotions had never been so aroused that she had contemplated marriage with any of them. Somehow she had always thought that she would know straightaway when the right man came along, but she hadn't even considered Rafe in that light at first, she had just been overwhelmingly grateful that he was willing to help her. But on the long days that they had spent alone together she had started to become aware of him as a man, and this awareness had magnified after the first time he kissed her. But, even then, she would probably never have fallen in love with him if she hadn't seen his bad leg and realised his vulnerability. Before she had been half afraid of him; he was so different from herself that he might almost have come from another world, not only of class and background, but of confidence and experience; he was a man in every sense of the word, while she was just a young, uninteresting nonentity. But the fact that he was vulnerable to pain, to frustration, to life, had brought him down to a level where she could fall head over heels in love with him.

And to tell him so, when he was holding her in his arms, had seemed the most natural thing in the world. Charis could no more have not said it than she could have not responded when he kissed her. But it was the strangest thing, because until she actually said the words she hadn't known herself that she was in love with him, but once they'd been spoken she knew that it was so and nothing could ever change it. All the more humiliating then to have it so swiftly rejected.

Charis lay very still in her bunk, trying desperately hard to be sensible about it, to reason things out. Just because she had fallen for Rafe it didn't mean that he was going to feel the same way. For all she knew he might be in love with someone else. But if that was so, a small voice in the back of her mind insisted, why, after he had pushed her away, had he said that he had known something like that would happen if they stayed in the trailer? Surely it could only mean that he had felt attracted to her and that if they were alone together in the trailer for any length of time he would be unable to resist making a pass at her. It would also explain why he had been so abrupt with her all that day. He had guessed that she was falling for him and wanted to avert just such a scene as had occurred. Only when it came to it he hadn't been able to prevent it because he couldn't resist making love to her. And that he should want her seemed the greatest miracle of all.

She sat up suddenly, her body hot and restless. She gripped the edge of the sleeping bag to stop her hands shaking and she could feel her heart racing in her chest. Although Rafe hadn't put it into words, he had given her a straight choice: she could have sex without strings, or nothing. And because he thought her the old-fashioned, romantic type, he had withdrawn rather than let her build up any false hopes. Being cruel to be kind, she supposed. And cruel to both of them, because she was sure that it must have cost him an effort to let her go when he wanted her. Dimly she realised that many men wouldn't have drawn back, they would have taken what they wanted and done the rejecting afterwards. For a few minutes she tried to work out why he was so against love and marriage, but his character was too complex for that, too much had happened in his past that she didn't know about. And besides, it was too difficult to concentrate when she felt so restless, so frustrated.

Bringing her legs up, Charis rested her head on her knees and gazed into the shadowy darkness, the room dimly lit by the moonlight that penetrated through the curtains. Rafe was only about fifteen feet away. Not more than a dozen paces. She had only to get up and take those few steps. And then he would reach for her and pull her down into his bed. Beads of perspiration

broke out on her forehead and Charis bit her thumb
hard, willing herself not to think about it. But her
whole body yearned for his touch, longed to be held
against his lean hardness. Trembling, Charis slipped
out of bed and stood up. Maybe learning to play Rafe's
game was preferable to spending the rest of her life
regretting what she had lost. Maybe settling for second
best was better than having nothing at all.

Slowly, tremblingly, Charis groped her way to the
door and softly opened it. It was darker in the main
body of the trailer, she had to stand for several
seconds in the doorway to let her eyes become accus-
tomed to it. Her hands were hot and slippery as she
gripped the door frame, and her heart was beating so
loudly that she couldn't hear Rafe's breathing. She
gulped and started on the few steps that would take
her to him. She was afraid, but the fire in her body
was fiercer than ever now and nothing would have
made her turn back.

His bed was in dark shadow, she could only make
out the outline of the double sleeping bag at its foot.
She moved nearer to the head of the bed and put out a
tentative hand. She opened her mouth to say his name,
but even as she did so she knew that the bed was
empty, that he wasn't there.

For a moment she was paralysed by shock and
couldn't move, then fear brought sensation rushing
back and her fingers scrabbled along the wall for the
light. She found it at last and switched it on, to have
the worst of her fears immediately allayed. It was all
right, he hadn't walked out on her, his things were still
here, neatly arranged, and the bed was made up ready
to be used. She sank down on the edge of the bunk,

relief making her legs feel suddenly weak. He must have gone for a walk, as unable to bear the tension of being so close to her and yet so far apart, as she had. Which meant ... But she was afraid to think of that; she couldn't. To have worked herself up enough to give herself to him and then find him gone had thoroughly unnerved her, and she was afraid of him finding her here when he came back, so she quickly turned the light out again and went back to her own room, there to lie awake until she heard the faint sounds he made when he returned an hour or so later, sounds so quiet that only someone who had been listening very intently would have heard them. With a long sigh, Charis relaxed at last and drifted off into sleep.

The third commune was neither so open as the farm nor as fenced in as the Hall had been, but it was definitely much harder to find. Even though the people Rafe had talked to in the pub had given him rough directions, it took them a couple of hours before they found the entrance. Two hours of driving round narrow country lanes that seemed to wind round in circles, climbing hillsides and joining other lanes that took them back where they started. There were never any signposts at the junctions they came to; presumably because the lanes didn't lead anywhere very much, and were only used by locals who knew where they were going anyway, so what was the point? Why put up signposts for any chance stranger who might venture along the maze of lanes just once in a blue moon? It would have saved time if Rafe had asked, of course, but he was reluctant to do so so close to the commune where a chance remark about strangers trying to find the place might reach the ears of one of the inmates.

At last they found what Rafe was sure must be the right place, although there was no signboard or anything else to tell them so.

When Charis pointed this out, he answered, 'It's the very fact that there isn't a nameboard that makes me think I'm right. Every other place along this road except this one has had a nameboard of some sort so that the postman knows where to deliver letters.'

'Yes, I think you're right.' Charis looked out of the car window at the small lodge house that stood on the right-hand side of a five-barred gate. Beyond the gate there was a cattle grid and a driveway that disappeared downhill among trees. There was a wire fence round the property that wouldn't keep even a dog out, but there were so many trees and bushes that it wasn't possible to see any building that lay beyond them.

'We'd better not linger here,' Rafe remarked as he drove on. 'There might be someone in the lodge house watching us.'

'How do we get in?' Charis asked him.

'We'll drive on for a bit and see if there's another gate.'

But it seemed that the one they had already seen was the only entrance, because after a while the wire fence gave way to a hedge behind which there was a neat farm. Rafe pulled up and they walked back up the hill.

'The first thing to do is to make certain we're right,' he told her when they came to the start of the wire fence and, presumably, the commune property. 'Wait here while I go and have a closer look.'

'I'm coming with you,' Charis objected.

'Charis . . .'

'I'm coming,' she told him firmly, and swung a determined leg over the fence.

'All right,' Rafe agreed resignedly. 'But keep behind me and do as you're told.'

He put a hand on one of the supports and sprang lightly over the fence to join her, then they made their way cautiously through the trees. The grounds weren't very well looked after; the undergrowth was thick and there were several fallen branches, with one or two whole dead trees that had fallen to the ground and were now almost lost among the bracken and moss. It wasn't a nice day for walking in thick woodland; the sky was grey and overcast as if it might soon rain and the place smelt dank and neglected, the trees growing too close together. They came to a stream that ran down the hill across their path and Rafe helped her over. Charis' hand quivered in his, but if he noticed it he gave no sign, letting it go as soon as she was safely across and turning to go on ahead of her.

Charis looked at his broad back unhappily. He had mentioned what had passed between them only once that morning. That was when they had got in the car and were just about to set out to look for the commune. Then, just as he was about to start the car, he had hesitated and without looking at her, said harshly, 'About what happened last night; I want to apologise. It was my fault entirely. I hope you weren't—too upset by it?'

And Charis, God help her, had given the only reply she possibly could give. 'No, of course not. Let's forget it, shall we?'

He had given a noncommittal grunt and started the car. And Charis had been afraid to look at him because she couldn't bear to see the relief on his face. She wondered what he would have said if he had known that she had gone to him, ready to give him anything he wanted.

The stream trickled down from an overgrown pond that might once have been part of an ornamental lake, for the ground some way round it was soft and slushy. Insects hovered in the damp undergrowth and there was a fetid air about the place. Charis shivered and moved closer to Rafe.

They had to go round in a wide circle to avoid the pond, and then Rafe headed uphill again. The trees thinned out a little and Charis noted that, whereas before most of the trees had been pines and other evergreens, now there were deciduous, ornamental trees with large neglected shrubs like purple and mauve rhododendrons. They ducked under the widespread branches of a willow and Rafe stopped so suddenly that Charis bumped into him.

'What is it?'

'Look for yourself.'

She peered round his shoulder and saw that ahead of them were the remains of what might once have been a landscaped garden with large open spaces of long grass between clumps of trees and shrubs. In the centre of the cleared space, occupying a large area, stood the ruins of what must once have been an extremely large house. Now, however, there were only the foundations and the uneven line of the lower parts of the walls left, with here and there a chimney rising higher. In some places creeper had overgrown the walls and it was evident that soon the place would go back to nature.

'A ruin? But I don't understand.' Charis looked at Rafe in some confusion. 'Have we come to the wrong place?'

'It looks like it,' he admitted ruefully. 'Perhaps that's why there was no name on the gate.' He looked carefully round then walked towards the ruins. 'This was evidently done some time ago, by the amount of weed that's growing over it,' he remarked as they got nearer. He pulled some of the weed off a portion of the wall and bent to have a closer look. 'From the way these bricks are blackened I'd guess it was a fire that did the damage. The place must have been burnt almost to the ground.'

'I wonder why no one rebuilt it; it must have been quite a place,' Charis surmised as she wandered through the ruin, trying to work out what the rooms must have been.

'Too expensive, I expect. It would have cost a small fortune just to insure a place this size adequately.' He straightened up and brushed his hands. 'We'd better get back to the car and start looking again. We've wasted enough time here.'

'Do we have to go back through the wood?' Charis asked, disliking the idea.

'No point. Look, there's the remains of a gravel track. Perhaps it was the drive up to the house and will bring us to the gate. We'll go that way.'

They set off, both being careful to keep a space between them so that they didn't accidentally touch. Charis stole a glance at Rafe, but saw only the sternness of his profile, the same withdrawal that had been in his face yesterday together with a new tightness about his jawline. Her own feelings and hopes she didn't try to analyse. It was as if she had put them away in a drawer until Jane was safe, only then would she have the time and courage to take them out again.

The drive was a long one, winding uphill away from the house, and soon they could no longer look back and see it or the open space around it. After they had covered a couple of hundred yards it came to a fork, but both paths were overgrown with weeds and there was no indication which led to the gate.

'We'll take this one,' Rafe decided, and followed the left fork through the trees, but this soon began to go downhill again and he murmured, 'Looks like we've taken the wrong one, but we'll go on a little farther.'

They came to a very high stone wall on one side, the mortar crumbling and weeds and flowers growing in the niches. Their feet made little noise on the overgrown path and the place was very quiet, there was only the sound of birdsong in the air. Then, quite clearly, they heard someone shout and they came to an abrupt stop.

'Carol!' The shout in a man's voice came again and they instinctively looked behind them, but there was no one there. Charis frowned and opened her mouth to ask Rafe where he thought it was coming from, but he put a finger to his lips and made a gesture towards the wall.

'Carol—don't you know what the time is?' The voice, exasperated now, but not so loud, came nearer. 'You know we want those beans for lunch.'

'Well, I'm going as fast as I can. Nearly all the beans near the ground have been picked and I can't reach the high ones.'

The answering voice was so close that it startled

them; its owner must have been standing only a yard or so away on the other side of the wall.

'Here, I'll help you.' The man must have joined the woman, because his voice had dropped quite considerably.

Rafe motioned to Charis to stay still and, being careful where he put his feet so as not to step on any gravel, moved over against the wall to hear better. Charis immediately disobeyed and joined him.

'How many beans do we need?' the man was asking.

'The whole basketful; they want some for tonight as well. There are going to be about six extra to dinner tonight.'

'Because of the mating ceremony?'

'Yes, some of the elders are coming.'

The gist of that remark hit Charis and she gasped and made a grab at Rafe to attract his attention. But he was before her and quickly put a hand over her mouth to stop her making any noise. His eyes were bright with excitement, mirroring her own.

'I remember my first mating,' the man was saying. 'Nervous as a cat, I was. It was almost like being married in a church. Only in some ways it was worse; with the girls all rigged up in that veil thing they put on her and not knowing who the elders had picked for me.'

'How many mates have you had since?'

'Three. And I got them all pregnant,' the man added proudly. 'I've given five kids to the family now.'

Charis' eyes widened and Rafe's hand tightened warningly. The man and the woman were silent for a while and all they could hear was the rustle of the leaves on the runner bean plants that were obviously growing against the other side of the wall. They started to talk about some other people then, names that meant nothing to the two listeners, but presently the woman said, 'That should be enough, the basket's nearly full.'

'Okay.'

The voices moved away and Rafe quickly turned and ran along beside the wall, keeping to the grass. Charis followed him, her pulses racing, afraid of making a noise but even more afraid of missing something. At the corner of the wall Rafe stopped and looked carefully round. Not able to go past him for fear of being seen, Charis dropped to her knees and peered past his legs. The track they were on went round the corner and a few feet along to a wooden gate in the high wall, but once past the gate the track was no longer overgrown, it was clean shingle, showing that it had plenty of use. The voices came nearer again and Rafe dodged back, almost falling over Charis. He glared at her and pulled her back out of sight.

'. . . at least three chickens for tonight,' the woman's voice was saying.

'This girl that's to be mated,' the man asked curiously. 'Have you seen her yet?'

'No, no one's seen her since they brought her two days ago. She's been shut in her room and we won't see her until we dress her for the ceremony.'

'Who's the man the elders have chosen?'

But the woman's reply was lost as the gate banged shut on its hinges and the gravel scrunched under their feet as they walked along the track.

Charis chanced a look and saw only their back views; a dark-haired man in working clothes and a small, plump girl in jeans and sweater.

Rafe put his hand on her collar and hauled her back. Charis got to her feet, her face white, and they stood together without speaking until everything was quiet again. Then Charis said in a strained voice, 'That was Jane they were talking about, I know it was.'

'Possibly.' He didn't attempt to deny it. 'But what a stroke of luck overhearing them, especially before they heard us. Let's take a closer look.' He moved forward to peer in at the gate, then came back to her. 'It looks like an old kitchen garden. Probably built to service that burnt-down mansion.'

'But where's the commune, then?'

'That's something we'll have to find out. Let's follow the track and see where it goes. And *this* time,' he added threateningly, 'you'll do as you're told. If it really was Jane they were talking about the smallest mistake on our part might lose our chance to help her. Understood?'

He looked at her gravely and Charis nodded. 'All right, I'll do as I'm told.'

'Good.' Carefully he crossed the track and walked along the grass parallel to it, using the trees as a screen and detouring round any open spaces.

The path led downhill all the way, but meandered in wide sweeps to the right through the trees. Faintly ahead of them they could hear the crunch of gravel and the murmur of voices as the man and woman preceded them. Presently the trees began to thin out and they moved more cautiously, then Rafe stopped, his body hidden by the trunk of a large oak and Charis crept up behind him.

'Can you see it?'

'Yes.' He dropped down to his knees and pulled her

down beside him. 'Have a look, but be careful.'

Charis peered round the trunk and at first couldn't see anything, but then she looked between two bushes lower down on the slope and gave a gasp of astonishment. At the foot of the hill stood a building, white-walled and so strangely ornamented that for a few minutes she could only stare at it incredulously. The building itself wasn't very large and seemed to form two sides of a square, but with the main part two storeys higher than the second. The other two sides of the square were formed just by a very high wall, but at each corner of the square there were tall round turrets, too small in diameter to be a room, capped with green tiles that must once have sparkled in the sun but now looked dull and lacklustre. In the centre of the wall facing them was a large arched entranceway, barred by a heavily decorative wrought-iron gate. Above the gateway there were more turrets, and the roof of the house itself was also castellated and adorned with a large dome.

'Good heavens!' Charis exclaimed in a whisper. 'It looks like the Sleeping Beauty's castle!'

'Which may be more accurate than you think,' Rafe returned. 'It certainly looks as if some eccentric decided to embellish the place. It was probably quite a decent Georgian house before he got to work on it.' He studied the place for a while longer, then said, 'You know, I think this must probably have been the coach-house and stables for the mansion. You see those low buildings on the far side, they look as if they've been converted from stables to rooms.'

'What about the house, then?' Charis demanded. 'Who would have lived there?'

'Probably the estate manager and his family.' Suddenly he caught hold of her and pulled her closer into the tree trunk. 'Quiet, someone's coming.'

A man came out of an old barnlike building lower down the slope, but above the house. He was leading two goats by pieces of rope attached to collars round their necks and set off, whistling, up the path back towards the walled garden.

'He must tether them up there somewhere,' Rafe observed after he had gone by. 'We must be careful not to run into them on the way back.' He paused, then said, 'Listen. Do you hear anything?'

Charis tilted her head. A faint, regular rumbling sound carried faintly to her. 'You mean that sort of humming noise?'

'Yes. I think it's coming from one of those outhouses. I'm going to go down and take a closer look. If I circle back through the trees I should be able to keep the outhouses between me and the house and not be seen.' He started to move off, then stopped and looked at her. 'I can trust you not to follow me this time, can't I?' He was still crouched down beside her, his face very close.

Charis nodded, not letting herself look into his eyes. 'Yes, I'll stay here.'

'Good girl!'

He turned and slipped away through the trees. Charis watched him go and wondered why such a small, casual compliment should make her feel as if he'd given her all the treasures of the world. She turned to watch the house again and settled down to wait. There was quite a lot of activity about the place; cars drove up twice and pulled up on the gravelled drive in front of the house, but they didn't go through the ornamental gateway, their occupants got out and rang a bell attached to the wall and someone came out of the house to open the gate and let them walk through. Some children came out to play in the courtyard, their voices high-pitched and happy, their feet making a lot of noise in the loose shingle with which the courtyard seemed to be covered. Charis wondered whether they ever went to school like normal children, or whether the members of the Brotherhood taught them themselves, together with their religious dogma, of course. And were any of them one of the five children that the man they had overheard had sired for the 'perfect family' as the Brotherhood believed themselves to be?

Rafe was back much sooner than she expected; she had been watching carefully but hadn't seen him enter any of the outhouses. He motioned her to follow him and they retreated back into the thicker trees where there was no possibility of being seen from the house.

'The noise came from a generator,' he told her tersely. 'There can't be any electricity laid on here and they have to generate their own.'

'How do you know?' Charis asked him. 'I didn't see you go into any of the sheds.'

'They have windows at the back, luckily. The other sheds are used for storage mostly: animal feeds, fuel, that kind of thing.' He paused and looked at her. His voice gentle, he said, 'You realise, Charis, that if they were talking about Jane, which I must admit seems very likely, then they intend to put her through this mating ceremony tonight, don't you?'

Charis nodded and looked at him anxiously. 'Poor Jane! What are we going to do?'

He grinned, the devilish gleam back in his eyes. 'Why, get her out first, of course.'

CHAPTER NINE

'Oh, Rafe!' Hope filled her heart again and she put out a hand towards him, then she remembered and hastily drew it back, her face flushing. Rafe's brows drew into a frown, so she said quickly, 'Have you decided how you're going to do it?'

'Not yet. Unfortunately we can't do much until it gets dark, especially about trying to locate which room Jane is in. About all we can do is to look over the place a bit more and find out how to get from the commune to the road. There might be a chance of driving the car nearer.'

They spent the next couple of hours cautiously exploring and found that the gravel track went past the house and then turned uphill again for about half a mile before it came to the lodge house beside the lane. Rafe looked it over carefully, then shook his head. 'We haven't a chance of bringing the car past here,' he told her regretfully. 'Not only would you have to get the gate open, but it would make such a racket going over the cattle grid that it would be sure to alert anyone inside, and you can bet your life they'd come out to investigate or else telephone a warning to the main house. No, I'm just going to have to carry her out, which might not be easy if she's struggling to get free or to scream.' He looked at Charis rather questioningly. 'I may have to tie and gag her.'

'Of course, if you have to,' Charis agreed with ruthless disregard for her sister's feelings. 'But it may not be necessary. You remember when I saw her being brought here in their van? Well, she was looking through the window, and I'm quite sure that she saw me. But the strange thing was that she didn't instantly recognise me; she just sort of stared at me as if she wasn't quite sure who I was. And since then I've wondered if it was because she was drugged.'

She had kept her tone as even as she could, but Rafe looked at her sharply. 'And you've been worrying yourself sick about it ever since, I suppose. Why didn't you tell me before?' he demanded roughly.

'You weren't in a very conversational mood yesterday,' she answered levelly.

He was silent for a moment, then swore. 'Hell and damnation!' Catching hold of her arm, he said urgently, 'Look, if they've found it necessary to drug her it can only be because she's seen through the Brotherhood and doesn't want to stay in it. She might even have tried to get away herself and that's why they put her in the Hall with its high walls and gate. Then again, she might not have been drugged at all, they might just have given her tranquillisers to keep her quiet during the journey. And that would make it better for us, because it will be a hell of a lot easier to get her out if she comes with us willingly.'

Lifting her head, Charis smiled at him rather tremulously. 'There seems to be an awful lot of ifs and mights in what you said I only hope you're right.' She glanced down to where his hand still lay on her arm and moved it away. His eyes came up to look at her, but she wouldn't meet them, turning her head away. 'What's the time?'

'Almost three,' he told her. 'Still another six hours before we can make a move.'

'What shall we do, wait here or go back to the car?'

'Stay here, I think. I'm going to circle round the back of the house and see if I can spot where they're keeping Jane. I'm going to leave you here and I want you to try and get some sleep; if we get Jane out we'll have to go straight back to the caravan, collect our stuff, and then head for the nursing home in Kent, and I'll want you to do some of the driving.'

'Couldn't we stay in the caravan tonight?'

He shook his head. 'It would be too risky. It would only take a visit to the local Tourist Information Office with your description, for them to get on to our trail. And once they got your sister back I don't think we'd have much chance of getting to her a second time.'

He watched her crawl under the cover of a rhododendron bush, then left her again. Charis tried to sleep but couldn't. Her mind kept going back to Rafe, but that way led only to wretchedness, so she resolutely turned her thoughts back to Jane. When Rafe returned an hour or so later he told her that he thought he'd worked out which was Jane's room. 'It's on the first floor in the main building, and there's a ladder long enough to reach it in one of the sheds. Maybe our luck's changing at last,' he told her with a grin.

It seemed to take forever before it was dark enough for them to make a move. They had waited together under the dimness of the flowering shrub and neither had spoken very much. Rafe had slept for some time; he seemed to have the ability to fall asleep at the drop of a hat and wake exactly at the right time, as if he had some sort of inner alarm clock. Crawling out of their hiding place, they slowly and carefully made their way back towards the commune. Charis was glad now that the day was a dull one, it made the evening that much darker and there was little chance of a moon. There were a few lights on in the house, mainly downstairs, but there was no one about; it wasn't the sort of evening when people sat outdoors.

'Follow me, and be as quiet as you can,' Rafe instructed. He led her down the hillside towards the outhouses but off to the left so that they came out at the back of them. The hum of the generator was louder now, like the steady pulse of a heartbeat.

'Stay here,' he whispered in her ear. 'I'm going to go round and get the ladder and pass it through the window of the shed to you. Don't try and carry it, just take the weight and lower it to the ground. And whatever you do don't drop it.'

'No, Major,' Charis agreed in meek obedience that didn't fool him for a minute. He laughed softly and melted into the shadows again.

Ten minutes later the window above her head creaked slowly open and he passed the end of the ladder through. It was difficult to get it out silently; the window aperture was small and the ladder had to be lifted and guided through from both ends to prevent it scraping noisily against the frame. Twice wood rasped against wood and they froze and waited breathlessly in case someone had heard them, but eventually it was through and Charis was able to take Rafe's end from him and lay it on the grass until he rejoined her.

'Okay?'

'Yes.'

'Right. Now I want you to go ahead of me to make

sure the coast's clear. If you see anyone run back and tell me. We'll have to return the way we came and circle round to the back of the house. We can't risk going by the converted stable block in case someone looks out of the window and sees us.'

Rafe lifted the ladder and they set off, but it took quite a while to make the long trek round again. The back of the house was painted white like the front, but there were several climbing roses and other creepers that relieved the starkness of the walls.

'Which window?' Charis whispered.

'The one at the far end.'

'How do you know it's the right one?'

'I don't, but it's the only one that isn't open to air the room. If it's the wrong one we can at least try to get in there.'

They crept down towards the house, carrying the ladder between them now, and crouching down low in case anyone looked out of one of the lighted windows on the ground floor. When they reached the house, Rafe lifted the ladder and placed it gently against the wall. It came just short of the windowsill. Motioning Charis to hold the bottom, Rafe began to climb. The ladder was wooden and rather old, its timbers creaked and groaned as Rafe put his weight on the rungs and Charis' heart was in her mouth as she looked anxiously at the lighted windows, certain that somebody would hear.

But Rafe reached the top safely and took a knife out of his pocket to force the latch. Then he climbed over the sill and disappeared inside. Charis stared upwards, her heart in her mouth, as terrified for Rafe as for her sister. He was inside for what seemed like ages but was

really only a couple of minutes, then his head appeared
through the window and he beckoned her to come up.
Gingerly Charis began to climb, holding the rungs
tightly. She had never liked heights and had no trust
whatsoever in the safety of the ladder, but if Rafe
needed her nothing on earth would have stopped her
from reaching him. At the top, he caught hold of her
and lifted her almost bodily across the sill. The room
behind him was in semi-darkness with no artificial light
at all, and for a moment she thought that he'd been
wrong and the room was empty, but then he gestured
silently towards the corner and Charis saw a girl
crouching there, her arms up to protect herself, her
eyes large and frightened.

'Jane!' Charis flew across the room and knelt beside
the quivering figure. 'Jane, don't you know me? It's
Charis. Look, darling, look!'

Behind her she heard Rafe whisper, 'I'll close
the curtains, then we'll risk a light. She was frightened to death when I came through the window.' He
drew the curtains, then switched on a small bedside
lamp.

Charis looked at Jane and gently reached out to
touch her hand. Immediately the hand was snatched
away, but Charis talked quietly to her sister, telling
her not to be afraid. 'Don't you recognise me, darling?
It's Charis. I've come to take you home.' While all the
time her heart was bleeding inside at her sister's thin-
ness, the great shadows round her eyes, at the way she
trembled with fright.

'Charis?' The word was said so softly, so unsteadily
that for a moment she couldn't believe she'd heard it,
but then Charis' face lit with a wonderful smile and

the next moment she had taken her sister in her arms and they were both crying.

'Is—is it really you?' Wonderingly Jane put up her hand to touch her sister's face. 'I thought you came before, but it was just a dream.'

'Well, it isn't a dream this time,' Charis assured her firmly. 'I'm taking you home. And look,' she indicated Rafe who was standing silently by, 'a friend has come with me. You mustn't be afraid of him, darling. He's going to help us.'

Jane looked at them both and began to cry again. Charis helped her up and sat her on the bed, trying to calm her. 'We ought to get out of here as soon as we can,' Rafe reminded her.

'Yes, all right.' Charis went down on her knees and took hold of Jane's hands. 'Darling, don't cry any more. We're going to go now and we want you to be very quiet, as quiet as when we used to play at hide and seek at home together. Do you remember?' She spoke as if to a young child, because that seemed the only level at which her sister was able to understand at the moment.

Slowly Jane stopped crying, and they got her into a jacket Charis found in the wardrobe, and over to the window.

'I'll take her down first,' Rafe told her, 'then hold the ladder while you climb down. Turn off the light.'

Charis moved to obey him. Experimentally she tried the door and wasn't at all surprised to find it locked. She went over to help Jane climb out of the window, whispering words of encouragement as Rafe began to guide her down. But a noise in the corridor outside caught her attention and she ran over to the door again. Faintly she heard the sound of women's voices coming nearer. Frantically she ran over to the window, ready to climb out and follow Jane and Rafe. But then she hesitated; if she did that and the women came into the room they would be bound to see the ladder and give the alarm before they had time to get away. With Jane to slow them down they would be caught for sure. Without giving herself time to think any further, Charis closed the window as quietly as she could, then ran across to lie on the bed with her back to the door. She and Jane were wearing similar clothes, denims and a sweater, with the room in semi-darkness as it was, anyone looking in to check might mistake her for Jane.

She lay there with beating heart as the voices came close, then a key was inserted in the lock and the women came in.

'She's lying here in the dark,' one remarked, and switched on the light.

Someone came over and shook her, not unkindly. 'Come on, dear, it's time to get ready.' Charis didn't move and the woman shook her again. '*Come on,*' she insisted. 'You're not that tired, you've had plenty of time to sleep during the past two days.'

Charis had to move, there was no point in trying to hold out any longer, but even so she put her hands up in front of her face as if the light hurt her as she slowly turned over, expecting any minute for the women to give a startled shout and raise the alarm. But the women merely pulled her to her feet and took her out of the room and down the corridor a little way to a bathroom. At first Charis couldn't believe that they hadn't realised she wasn't Jane, but then she remembered what the woman in the kitchen garden had said: that Jane had been kept in her room and no one had seen her since she arrived, and she gave a great inner sigh of relief. They thought she was Jane, and so long as they went on thinking that it would give Rafe more time to get her sister away. She could imagine the surprise he must have got when she closed the window, but he was quite sharp-witted enough to have guessed what had happened and to get Jane to safety before he came back for her. But in the meantime she must try and act just like Jane would have done.

One of the women, all of them in their late twenties or early thirties, was running a bath and another was trying to undress her. Charis involuntarily pulled away and the woman said, 'Now then, you want to be all nice and clean for the ceremony, don't you?' and proceeded more firmly to take off Charis' sweater.

If I go along with them, Charis thought, they'll leave me alone to have a bath and I might be able to sneak back to the room and down the ladder. So she let them undress her, but instead of leaving her alone they helped her to wash herself, a process that Charis found acutely embarrassing. Then they wrapped her in a bathrobe and took her back to Jane's room, where they began this time to dress her in all white underwear and a long white dress like a wedding dress. They hadn't bothered to close the curtains and Charis couldn't help wondering if Rafe had got back and was up the ladder watching what was going on, but she didn't dare look towards the window to find out in case she attracted the women's attention to it. She was also getting increasingly worried. What if she wasn't left alone long enough to get away? What if they took her down to the mating ceremony and one of the Brotherhood realised she wasn't Jane? What the hell happened at this mating ceremony anyway?

One of her worries was slightly allayed when, after they had brushed out her hair, they arranged a long heavy veil over her head. Then she was given a book to carry with the Brotherhood's full title printed in gold on the cover, and which she guessed must be their version of a prayer book. By now she was so nervous that she was shaking, which must also have helped the women to believe that she was Jane.

When she was ready to their satisfaction, the three women led her out of the room and down the corridor to a staircase. This led down to a sort of ante-room where some men were waiting. One of them was bearded and wore a long white robe with some sort of emblem embroidered in gold on it, and Charis guessed that this must be one of the elders of the sect. He carried a metal staff in his hand and looked at her searchingly as she was brought down the stairs. Charis cowered behind the veil, glad of its thick folds although she could scarcely see through them.

'Jane?' the elder said. When she didn't answer he looked at the women. 'Is she ready?'

'Yes, but she's very nervous,' one replied.

The sound of singing came from the other side of the double doors that led out of the room. Lifting up his staff, the elder banged on the doors three times. The sound of singing increased as the doors slowly opened, then he took her hand and led Charis forward into the room. There seemed to be a great many people there, all singing and wearing bright clothes and with flowers in their hair, the men as well as the women. At the end of the room was a sort of altar with another elder standing in front of it. Charis drew back and looked round wildly, but the man gripped her hand firmly and pulled her forward. Rafe, Charis prayed, Rafe, for heaven's sake come and get me out of this!

But she was led inexorably on, then made to kneel in front of the altar. Someone came to kneel beside her, but she didn't dare look up to see who it was. One of the elders began a long intonation, speaking in a dry, monotonous voice. There was singing and then more words. She was made to stand up, then kneel down again, and to repeat some words after the elder. The ceremony was very long and Charis grew ever more desperate. It occurred to her that the elders probably knew Jane quite well from when she had been at the headquarters in Bristol, and it also occurred to her that at some point in an ordinary wedding ceremony the bride was required to lift her veil. If they did that here ... Growing panic hit her as she wondered what on earth to do. Should she pretend to faint, or throw a screaming fit? She had just decided on the latter when all the lights went out.

For a moment everyone was taken by surprise, including Charis, then she turned and plunged through the darkness back towards the doors. But the man who had been standing beside her must have felt her move and caught hold of her arm. Nearby someone groaned and said, 'The generator's packed up again.' Desperately Charis tried to break free of the man's hold, but he laughed and put an arm round her.

'Don't be afraid,' the man said, his English heavily accented. 'See, we soon have light.'

And someone was, in fact, using a torch to help others who were lighting candles. There seemed to be quite a few of these standing ready in the room, so the generator breaking down must have been a regular event. Charis again tried to get free but the man held her firmly and she looked at him for the first time. He was about forty, as far as she could judge in the dim light, and had long light brown hair and a beard. He was quite tall, and this, together with his accent, made her guess that he came from one of the Scandinavian countries.

The ceremony went on and at the end they lifted off her veil, but the light was so dim now that the elders couldn't see the superficial differences that set her apart from her sister, they saw only a girl of the same height and the same colouring, and didn't look close enough into her face to see the rest. At the end the man she had been given to as a mate put a wreath of flowers on her head and Charis was given one to do the same to him. Then all the members of this strange congregation crowded round them, giving them flowers to hold or slipping garlands over their heads. Taking her hand, the man led her towards the double doors, and fear rose in her throat again as she wondered what on earth was going to happen next. Somehow she had to get out of this *now*, before it was too late, but there were people all around her and there was just no way out.

They walked through the double doors with people still singing and giving them flowers. Many of them kissed her, too, or wished her happiness in her mating. The women who had got her ready came up to them and Charis expected that they, too, would offer felicitations, but instead they took her hands and led her away from all the others, and from the Scandinavian, who stood alone looking after them, a wide grin on his face. Charis went with them willingly enough, glad of anything that might give her a chance to get away. They took her down a short corridor, then through a door that opened on to the courtyard. She recognised where she was as soon as she saw the turrets at the corners of the walls looming whitely against the darkness of the night.

It came to her that if she was going to escape this might be her last chance, and she jerked her arms free from the women on either side of her. She began to run towards the gate, but her long skirts impeded her and her feet slipped noisily on the loose pebbles with which the courtyard was covered. The women had no difficulty in catching her again and held her more firmly than ever.

'Don't be silly,' one of them scolded. 'There's nowhere to run to. We're your family now; your old family doesn't want you any more. You know that, you were told before. Now, come on,' a woman encouraged, 'Karl is going to look after you from now on. And you don't want to keep him waiting, do you?'

They more or less dragged her across the courtyard to the converted stables and into the end door. To Charis' surprise the place was quite pleasant; there was a sort of hall with a bathroom opening off it, but she didn't see much of this because they hustled her into a bedroom beyond it. Here, by the light of an oil lamp, she saw that the old stable walls had been brushed clean so that the deep, rich red of the bricks gave a warm glow to the room, but the far wall had been clad in pine and against this was set a large double bed with a gay patchwork quilt. There wasn't much furniture in the room, just a solid-looking chair and a small stripped pine chest of drawers, but an effort had been made to embellish the place with lots of flowers set in vases round the room, and woven hangings on the walls.

But Charis took little notice of her surroundings, she turned to the women and said, her voice urgent and pleading, 'Please, don't leave me here! I don't want to go through with this. Please help me!'

But she might just as well have spoken to stone statues. They made her take off her clothes, using force when she tried to struggle, deaf to all her pleas, and then made her put on a white robe similar to that of the elders, with strange emblems embroidered on it, but in red this time. They treated her roughly, especially after she accidentally hit one of them in her struggles.

'We'll have to tell them to give her some more pills,' the eldest of the women panted as she tried to pull the robe over Charis' head. 'She was supposed to be kept quiet.'

After that Charis didn't struggle so much, fearful of losing her will to escape if they did as they threatened. When they had got her into the robe, the women picked up the discarded clothes and left her alone, locking the door behind them. Immediately she began to feverishly look for a way out, but the window was barred and anyway gave on to the courtyard with its tell-tale pebbles, and the door was too solid to even attempt to break down even though she threw herself at it and shook it furiously.

With a sob of despair she gave up, knowing that it was hopeless; they would never have left her alone here if there had been any chance of getting out. She would just have to wait until that man they called Karl came here to claim his rights. And then ... and then ... Clearly she heard the sound of a door opening, of people calling out and laughing, then the door closed again and someone began to crunch across the pebbles towards her room.

Charis shot to her feet and looked wildly round, determined to put up some sort of a fight. Grabbing the chair, she carried it over to the door, threw the flowers from one of the larger vases on the floor and turned out the lamp before climbing up on to the chair, the heavy vase raised high in the air, ready to bring it down on Karl's head the moment he walked into the room.

The footsteps came nearer and she could hear him humming a tune as he walked. Her grip on the vase tightened, as did the determined line of her mouth. She remembered her sister's scared, thin face and knew no mercy for a man who was willing to debauch a girl whose will-power to resist had been taken from her. The footsteps stopped and the man was quiet. Despite herself Charis' hands began to tremble as she wondered why he was waiting. Oh, Rafe, where the hell are you? Her mind flew to the man she loved, longing for his strength, his protection. The footsteps started again and she knew that she was on her own, no one else could help her now.

CHAPTER TEN

THE crunch of footsteps on the gravel came up to the outer door, paused as a key was fitted in the lock, then the door opened and Karl stepped into the hall. Sweat broke out on Charis' forehead and her hands were so hot and slippery that she was petrified she would drop the vase and break it. He paused for a minute, then came to her door and turned the key. Charis raised the vase a few inches higher and brought it crashing down as he stepped through the door.

But he must have suspected something, because he immediately lifted up an arm to protect his head and ward off the blow. The vase smashed to pieces, but Charis didn't wait to see whether he had been hurt, she launched herself at him in an attempt to knock him out of the way and get through the door. He gave a gasping sort of grunt as she landed on him and staggered back in the doorway. Charis pushed him as hard as she could, at the same time hitting out with her fists and feet wherever she could make contact. He reeled back into the hallway and she pushed past him, heading for the outer door. But she had only taken two steps when somehow he recovered enough to spring after her and drag her back. Charis gave a sob of pure rage and turned on her tormentor, tearing into him with her nails.

They fought silently except for Charis' sobs and snarls of anger and his winded gasps as he strove to get his breath back. She felt the material of her robe tear across the shoulders as he strove to restrain her and the sound made her fight harder than ever, but then he caught first one of her wrists and then the other, forcing them down behind her. Her strength was nearly gone, she knew that, but still she arched her back and tried to butt him with her head.

'You—little tigress!' The words were gasped out as he jerked his head out of the way. He took her wrists in one hand and with the other reached up to grab a handful of her hair, forcing her to be still. After a couple more rasping breaths he said, his voice more normal and achingly familiar, 'You little fool, it's me!' Then he roughly pulled her to him and kissed her.

For a few frozen seconds Charis' mind was too paralysed to accept it, but then she felt Rafe's lips on her mouth, seeking a response, and she gave him a great sigh of thankfulness and tore her arms free to fling them round his neck, kissing him back with enough fervour almost to knock him off his feet again.

'Hey!' He lifted his head up, his eyes laughing at her in the half-light. 'Give me a chance to get my breath back! You knocked the stuffing out of me when you jumped on me!'

'Oh, Rafe!' She clung to him, all inhibitions forgotten in the enormity of her escape, kissing his chin, his cheek, his neck, anything she could reach, while tears of relief ran down her cheeks. 'I didn't think you were coming. And I was so afraid. All through that dreadful ceremony I prayed that you would come for me. But you didn't, and I thought—I thought . . .'

'It's all right. Oh, my darling girl, it's all right.' He held her trembling body very close, letting her cry out her fear and shock on his shoulder, then led her gently through the debris of the broken vase into the bedroom, shouldering the door shut behind them. Sitting her down on the bed, he went back to lock the door, then lit the lamp before coming to sit beside her and take her in his arms.

But by now her brain had begun to work again and Charis sat up with a jerk. 'Rafe! The man Karl, he'll be coming here any moment. We've got to get away before he comes!'

She tried to jump to her feet, but Rafe held her down, 'No one's coming here,' he told her, adding with a grim look to his mouth, 'especially the man they wanted to give you to.'

'But . . .'

He stopped her words with a kiss. 'I told you he's not coming. I took care of him.' And he couldn't resist kissing her again as her mouth formed into an O of wonder.

'You did? How?'

'Never mind. Suffice it to say that he won't be seducing any more young girls for quite some time,' Rafe told her harshly.

Charis stared at him for a moment, then said vehemently, 'Good! I'm glad.'

He laughed aloud. 'You bloodthirsty little devil! I ought to have let him come in here so that you could have hit him with that vase. I've an idea that would have given you a great deal of satisfaction.'

'Yes, it would,' Charis agreed feelingly. 'And there are several of the others I would like to have hit too.'

He laughed again, then drew her to him and kissed her, long and lingeringly. Afterwards they were both silent until Charis said anxiously, 'Jane! I'd forgotten all about her. Where is she? Is she all right? We must go to her at once.'

She tried to get up again, but he held her still. 'Jane's fine. She's curled up on the back seat of the car, fast asleep. The walk there tired her out. And she's quite safe, all the doors are locked. I made sure of that before I came back to find out what had happened to you.' He lifted a hand to touch her cheek. 'That was quite something—staying to take Jane's place so that I could get her away.'

Charis shook her head impatiently. 'She's my sister and I love her. Anyone else would have done the same.'

'You're wrong. Not everyone else has the capacity to love like you do.'

His arm tightened around her and she nestled her head against his shoulder. But after a few minutes she said tentatively, 'Er—don't you think we ought to be getting out of here?'

He grinned. 'I wondered when you'd get round to that again. I think we'd better let things settle down a bit first. There are quite a few of them going backwards and forwards to try to fix the generator just now.'

'Oh, I was so thankful when that broke down. I was afraid that I'd have to lift my veil and they'd realise I wasn't Jane.'

'I know. That's why I decided to sabotage it.'

'You did that? Oh, Rafe, you are *brilliant*,' Charis told him fervently.

'I can't argue with that,' he agreed smugly. 'Now, how are we going to pass the time while we're waiting?'

Her voice strangely unsteady, Charis answered, 'What do you suggest?'

'Well, as the Brotherhood has been kind enough to supply us with a bed, it would be a shame not to make use of it, now wouldn't it?' and he gently pushed her down on to the pillows and lay down beside her. He kissed her gently, too gently, and Charis impatiently put her hand in his hair and kissed him back with a passion and desire as fierce as any he had shown. At first he was taken by surprise, but then his shoulders hunched as his own hunger caught fire and he took command, kissing her with uncontrolled eagerness.

It was quite some time before either of them had breath to speak, but then Rafe said thickly, 'I got more than I bargained for then, didn't I?'

Picking her words carefully, Charis said slowly, 'Maybe I'm not so old-fashioned as you think.'

'What does that mean?'

'It means that I love you. That I know you're not interested in marriage, but that I'm willing to accept just whatever you want to give of yourself.'

Rafe was silent for a long time, then he rolled off her and sighed. 'Dear God, I don't deserve that.' Then, 'I guess there comes a time for every man when he looks at himself and is ashamed of what he sees. And I'm certainly doing that now.'

'Rafe?' Charis raised herself on one elbow and looked at him questioningly.

There was a tight, set look to his face and a sort of weariness around his eyes, but this lessened as he turned his head to look at her. His hand came up to twine itself in her hair, then, abruptly, he said, 'I was a career soldier, Charis. All my life I wanted nothing

more than to be in the Army. Oh, there were women,
several of them over the years, and one or two I contemplated marrying. But the Army was my first love
and I wouldn't let anything interfere with that. Then,
early this year,' he went on, his voice slowing and full
of remembered pain, 'my regiment was sent to Ireland.
I was out on patrol near the border in an armoured
car, and we went over a mine. I was lucky, all I got
was a mangled leg. Most of the others were killed, or
so badly injured that they would have been better off
dead. It was quite some time before anyone came to
find us, and all I could do was lie there and listen to
my men . . .'

'Don't!' Charis threw herself down on to him and
held him tightly. 'Please don't go on.'

His hands came up to grip her arms and she could
feel them shaking. But after a moment he said, 'No, I
want you to hear it all. After they patched up my leg
they offered me a desk job, but I'm a field officer and
couldn't face spending the next twenty years sitting at
a desk. I told them I'd get the leg working as good as
new again, and they knew I'd do it too. So then they
told me the truth.' He smiled bitterly. 'They told me
that no matter how fit I was they would never put me
out in the field again. Because what had happened to my
men had made me too full of hate. They thought it would
cloud my judgment, and the political situations in countries where the Army is sent in are usually so knife-edge
that it was a risk they weren't prepared to take. So I had
no choice but to get out. Which left me at the ripe old age
of thirty-four with no career, no prospects, and only an
Army pension to live on,' he finished with embittered
irony. 'Hardly a catch for any woman.'

'Well, at least you're alive, aren't you?' Charis sat up in sudden anger. 'You're not a cripple, or blind! And you're a hell of a lot better off than a lot of people. You have a brain and you know how to use it. And look how you've helped me. If it hadn't been for you I'd never have got Jane out, and what's more . . .'

But she broke off, because he was laughing at her. Pulling her down to him, he looked up into her face and said softly, 'Oh, my darling girl, I love you so much. I can't fight the way I feel about you any longer. I tried, but I need you too much.'

After which they were both far too occupied to speak for several minutes. Then Rafe reluctantly let her go and sat up. 'I think it's time we left. They should have fixed the generator by now.'

Charis reached up to trace the outline of his jaw. 'Do we have to?'

He smiled and, catching her fingers, kissed them one by one. 'Yes, because you look extremely sexy with that nightdress thing falling off your shoulders, and if we go on as we were for much longer I'm going to have a great deal of difficulty in restraining myself. And this is neither the time nor the place.' Rolling off the bed, he went over to the window and carefully parted the curtains to look out. 'Yes, the electric lights are back on in the main house. It's safe for us to go.'

'I haven't any clothes to wear,' Charis reminded him. 'Or any shoes.'

'Here.' He peeled off his sweater and gave it to her. 'Bare feet won't matter in the grass and I'll carry you over any rough bits.' He turned out the lamp, then groped for her hand, 'Come on, darling, just this one last part in which we've got to be careful, and then it will be all over.'

Rafe led her into the hall and then, surprisingly, into the bathroom, where he slowly eased up the window which opened on to the outside of the courtyard.

'Isn't it locked?' Charis asked in a whisper.

'It was, but I saw them getting this place ready and fixed it earlier. That's why they locked you into the bedroom, I expect.'

When it was open high enough, Rafe stood on the side of the bath and climbed through, then Charis hitched up her skirt and followed him. He helped her down and they crept silently alongside the high wall that ran on the opposite side of the courtyard to the house. The night had cleared and a weak moonlight lit the way for them, but Charis was horribly aware that it might also give them away to anyone from the house once they left the protection of the wall. But only twenty yards from the end of the wall the outhouses started and they waited at the corner until a small cloud moved terribly slowly across the sky and obscured the moon before they chanced crossing the gap. As they went past the outhouses one of the goats must have heard or smelt them, because it began to bleat. Rafe swore under his breath, but then they were past and running as fast as they could into the welcoming cover of the trees.

After about ten minutes, they stopped, Charis panting for breath.

'Are your feet okay?'

'It's just—just the pine needles,' Charis managed gaspingly.

He knelt down and brushed off each of her feet, his

hands incredibly gentle, then he picked her up and carried her on through the woods.

It took them nearly half an hour to reach the car and, despite the danger, Charis thought it the happiest half hour of her life. She was held in the arms of the man she loved and he had said that he loved her in return; her sister was safe; no matter what the future held, this time would always be perfect.

Jane was still asleep as Charis slipped in beside her, leaving Rafe to drive them to the trailer where she swiftly dressed and collected their belongings. Rafe left a note together with the payment for the trailer, and then they began the long drive back into Kent. They didn't talk very much during the journey, although Rafe's hand often came down to cover hers as she sat beside him, his eyes proud and possessive. For a while she took the wheel as he sat, resting but watchful, beside her, but she had no trouble on the almost empty roads, with just a few long-distance lorries to pass as they drove on through the night covering almost the width of England.

They reached the nursing home in the early morning, but there was a porter on duty at the door who immediately sent for the resident doctor. By now Jane was awake and she clung to her sister, so that Charis went with her while the doctor examined her.

It was a couple of hours later before she came down again and found Rafe drinking a cup of coffee in a pleasant waiting-room overlooking the garden. He stood up as she came in and held out his hand to her.

'How is she?'

'She's fine. A bit weepy now that it's all over, but the doctor said that she hadn't been given any hard drugs, only strong sedatives, and with a lot of good food and rest, and constant reassurance, she should be perfectly okay in two or three months.'

'That's wonderful!' He smiled at her. 'Let's go for a stroll in the garden, shall we?'

The clear night had given way to a bright, sunny morning and it was pleasant to walk on the well-mani-cured lawn set among neat, geometrical flower beds. It seemed a far cry from the landscape Charis had got used to over the last couple of weeks: the rolling Malvern Hills and the beautiful green fields and valleys of the open countryside. Gardens were lovely, Charis decided, but how much more wonderful to have beautiful scenery as far as the eye could see, to have the whole countryside as your garden.

They walked through a trellised archway covered with yellow roses, out of sight of the windows of the nursing home, and then Rafe stopped and turned her to face him. 'You said that Jane is going to need con-stant reassurance; does that mean that you'll have to stay here with her?'

'No.' Shaking her head, Charis went on, 'They've told me not to in case she gets too dependent on me. But they want me to phone her every day and visit at the weekends. They want her to get well enough even-tually to go back to university, with someone there to keep a close eye on her, of course.'

'So you're free to do as you wish?'

'Yes, I suppose so,' she answered rather unsteadily, unable to look at him.

His hands came up to grip her arms and for once he seemed a little uncertain. Then he said roughly, 'I've already told you that I haven't much to offer you. But somehow, since last night, everything's changed. I feel, now, as if I could make a go of anything I turned my hand to. And I'm going to make damned sure that I do.' His eyes, so blue and clear, looked steadily into hers. 'So, my darling, will you risk taking me on?'

Charis gazed up at him, her answer already clear in her eyes, but she chose to tease him just a little. 'I thought you didn't like old-fashioned girls.'

'I don't as a rule. But when I thought about what that member of the Brotherhood intended to do to you, then I found I had some very old-fashioned notions of my own.'

'Really? Such as?'

He lowered his hands to her waist and drew her to him. 'Such as being jealous as hell of another man even touching you, let alone doing what he intended. And wanting to take care of you, and love you—always.'

'Oh, Rafe, that's all I'll ever want.'

And then they were kissing each other with fierce eagerness, until Rafe lifted Charis off her feet and swung her round, his face alight with happiness.

'We'll find ourselves a place in the country and breed horses or grow turnips, it doesn't matter what we do as long as we're together. I'll raise a loan and we'll start looking round tomorrow,' he told her exuberantly.

Charis laughed happily down at him. 'Hey, haven't you forgotten something? I still owe you for helping me to get Jane out.'

The devilish gleam that she loved came into his eyes. 'Ah, yes. I trust I did the job to your satisfaction, ma'am?'

'Most certainly.'

'In that case maybe you'll answer the question and tell me whether you'd consider taking me on in a permanent capacity.'

Charis looked lovingly down at him, and as she bent to kiss him, murmured, 'Speaking as an old-fashioned girl, I wouldn't have it any other way.'

Harlequin Plus
NAMES AND THEIR ORIGINS

The heroine of Sally Wentworth's delightful Presents has a beautiful and unusual name—Charis, which means "grace" in Greek. Many other first names, particularly women's, are derived from this ancient language, and we thought it would be interesting to gather a few of these and reveal their real meanings. . . .

Alexis	helper
Anthea	flowery
Chloë	young plant
Daphne	laurel
Eunice	great victory
Haidee	modesty
Nicola	victory of the people
Ophelia	help
Penelope	bobbin
Philippa	lover of horses
Phoebe	the shining one
Rhoda	rose
Sybil	prophetess
Tiffany	manifestation of God
Zoë	life